THE SCOUNDREL'S NEW CON

CATHERINE STEIN

Copyright © 2020 Catherine Stein, LLC.

All rights reserved. No part of this book may be used or reproduced by any means, graphic, electronic, or mechanical, including photocopying, recording, taping or by any information storage retrieval system without the written permission of the author except in the case of brief quotations embodied in critical articles and reviews.

This is a work of fiction. Names, characters, places, and incidents are products of the author's imagination or are used fictitiously. Any resemblance to actual events or persons, living or dead, is entirely coincidental.

ISBN: 978-1-949862-16-4

Book cover and interior design by E. McAuley:
www.impluviumstudios.com

To writers everywhere:
The world needs your stories. Let your voices shine.

Cast of Characters

Jack Weaver - A con man with an artistic side. Not to be trusted.

Tess Cochran - A journalist in search of the truth. Not trusting.

The Earl of Bardrick - A man of many trusts. Issuing a challenge.

Madame Xyla - A tepid medium.

Seance Guests - True believers.

Sir Cyril Montague, Lord Haverstock - Hangers on. Easily duped.

Lady Montague - A woman with a healthy passion.

Lady Virginia Farringdon - Hunting for ghosts, not a husband.

Rowland the Magnificent - Good with his hands.

Madame Le Fleur - Putting on a flowery act.

House Party Guests - Looking for a good show.

Spirits, Ghosts, and Spectres - Capriciously photogenic.

Bonaparte - A feline phantom.

1
The Magician

"*I'm* quite looking forward to the postmortal state, myself."

The young man who spoke those flippant words propped one arm up on the ornately-carved mantelpiece, lazily swirling a glass of brandy.

"After all," he continued, "who wouldn't want to spend eternity visiting lovely ladies in darkened chambers?"

He held Tess's gaze a moment more than was proper, his blue eyes dancing with merriment. He probably thought he could shock her. She was, after all, wearing a particularly plain and conservative mourning dress. The false spectacles would only add to the prim and proper illusion.

Tess answered his teasing smile with an unperturbed nod of her head. After three years as a journalist, she doubted much of anything could shock her. Certainly nothing at a mid-afternoon seance in a room full of middle-aged ladies dressed as primly as herself.

"I wouldn't be in any hurry to pass on to the next realm, were I you," she replied. "I'm certain we would all be the worse off for the lack of your presence, Mr.…?"

"Jack Weaver." He gave her a theatrical bow, his grin widening at her sarcastic retort. "Photographer for today's gathering. Delighted to make your acquaintance. Would you care to sit for a portrait?"

Mr. Weaver waved casually at the corner of the parlor. A worn sofa had been draped with a black shawl, and small tables to either side held ghoulish props and decorations. The sightless glass eyes of the taxidermy raven glinted in the light of a nearby candelabra. A camera stood at the ready, awaiting guests eager to capture their visit to this macabre gathering.

Tess made a mental note of the arrangement. Besides the raven, the tables held a skull, two bracelets of woven hair, an assortment of jet jewelry, a crystal ball, a deck of cards, and a book open to what looked like an astrological chart. When she had a private moment, she would record everything in her notebook.

"No, thank you, Mr. Weaver. I am here to engage with the spiritual realm, not to make a spectacle of myself."

As fun as it would be to have a photograph of herself, in any sort of costume, Tess couldn't take the risk someone might publish the photograph in a newspaper. Her editors required her to be discreet in her observations. If she were revealed to be a reporter, mouths and doors would close to her. And no story meant no pay.

Given her surroundings, she also suspected the fee for the photograph would be exorbitant.

Mr. Weaver abandoned his casual slouch and stepped toward her. "A true believer, are you?" His sandy-blond eyebrows raised in a skeptical arch. His right eye had a small patch of brown at the bottom of the otherwise-blue iris. Tess looked away so as not to stare.

"Indeed." Tess started toward the small group of women gathered at the opposite end of the room, taking refreshments to fortify themselves for the upcoming seance. "I'd thank you not to mock your prospective clients."

"No mockery was intended, Miss…"

"Mrs." Tess didn't look back. "Harris."

Weaver jogged to catch up to her vigorous strides. "Ah, of course. Here to contact your beloved husband, no doubt." His sympathetic tone contained a hint of cynicism. Apparently he didn't believe a word she said. Fitting, since she didn't believe a word he said, either.

"Yes. Poor Edgar," Tess sighed, acting now for the benefit of the other ladies.

"Tragic," Weaver replied. "Consumption, was it?"

"Typhoid fever."

He placed a hand over his heart. "The same illness that took my mother only last July. My deepest condolences, Mrs. Harris."

For the first time that evening, his words sounded sincere. Had he truly lost his mother to typhoid? Tess felt a stirring of guilt for choosing it as the killer of her fictional husband.

An older woman laid a hand on Weaver's arm, smiling sadly up at him. "Will you be joining us around the table, Mr. Weaver? You, too, deserve the chance to speak with those lost to you."

"It would be my pleasure, my lady."

Her face lit up. "Good boy. I'm so delighted. I am most eager to see if any spirits appear in the photographs you've taken this afternoon."

Weaver flashed perfect white teeth. "As am I, Lady Perkins. One can never say when or whom the spirits choose to visit, but with so many in attendance who wholeheartedly embrace the metaphysical, I must believe conditions favorable."

Tess's jaw tightened. He'd delivered that entire speech with the sincerity of a saint. The charlatan! These women weren't documenting their attendance at the seance. They'd paid good money in the hope of catching a glimpse of a loved one in a blurry ferrotype. Weaver was a spirit photographer. And his mother was probably alive and well.

Her fingers itched to pull out her notebook. She could expose him and Madame Xyla, all in one story. More visits would be necessary, along with research into photographic processes.

Tess turned to look Weaver in the eye again. How many

grieving people had he duped with that soothing baritone voice and charismatic smile? "What would you estimate the chances are of my dear husband appearing were I to sit for a portrait?"

"Given your recent loss and obvious attachment, I should say the odds are unusually high. But as I said, one never can know." His mouth twitched. He was mocking her again. "Would you like to sit? The entire process will take no more than fifteen minutes."

"I'm afraid I haven't any money with me today."

"Of course not. I can have the bill sent to your residence, as usual."

Tess gave him her sweetest smile. He probably didn't even tell his victims how much the fee was, the scoundrel. "I'd be delighted, Mr. Weaver. Thank you so much." She'd take the risk. A first-hand look at his methods would give her a good place to begin her investigation.

"Thank *you*, Mrs. Harris. I am only too happy to be of service to fellow believers."

"Or skeptics," she murmured as they walked together towards the camera. "Or anyone, really."

His smile didn't even falter. "It's so nice that we understand one another."

Mrs. Harris—or whatever her real name was—made a perfect photographic model. She didn't possess the dainty features so often believed feminine, but the play of light and shadow across her face highlighted elegant cheekbones and brilliant eyes. Jack hoped he could do her justice.

Despite the uncurtained windows and a number of lamps and candles around the room, the lighting wasn't ideal. It hadn't bothered him when he'd arranged everything. People who wanted spirit photographs expected them to be dark or hazy. Spirits didn't materialize in cheerful, sunlit gardens, after all. For his current customer, however, a garden on a cloudless day would be just the thing. In correct lighting, her features would show to their greatest advantage. Even the subtle freckling across her fair skin would be visible.

Today, unfortunately, he would have to make do with what he had. And he sure as hell wasn't going to make a spirit appear in her portrait.

He'd known her for a skeptic the instant she'd entered the room. He'd seen it in the slight narrowing of her eyes and the way she'd looked over the entire space with a calculated curiosity. If he'd been running a swindle on the street, he wouldn't have even attempted to catch her attention. There were plenty of easier marks to be had.

Now that he'd watched her a bit longer, he thought perhaps she might be an investigator. She was playing a role, that was certain. She'd responded to his initial banter the way a cynical young woman attending the seance at the behest of a friend might have done, then promptly declared herself a believer.

She'd also been poking around while he was in the darkroom preparing the plates. Instead of sitting on the sofa awaiting her photograph, she stood beside his array of props, flipping through his astronomy textbook with avid interest. Most people assumed the book had something to do with astrological predictions or they didn't bother to look at it in the first place. She probably knew exactly what it was. If he gave her enough time, perhaps she'd even discover which circulating library he'd stolen it from.

"Are you ready, Mrs. Harris?" he asked, readying the camera and adjusting the focus.

She looked up from the book and gave him an impish smile that made his heart give an odd little flutter. "Of course." She replaced the book on the table, smoothing the pages.

Jack eyed the astronomy text and nearly choked with laughter. This primly dressed widow had found the page where someone had doodled an obscene image in the margin and she'd displayed it for all to see. It seemed she had a mischievous streak. He quickly took the photo before her grin disappeared.

He wasted time repositioning the camera to capture her from another angle, which meant he'd need to be especially efficient at developing the photos before the plates dried. Also, he'd likely be late to the seance room, but the delay would be worth it if the photographs came out as he hoped. That glint in her eye and slight twist of her lips would be hanging on his wall of favorite photos soon, unless the damned lighting ruined it. He took his final exposure and scurried into the darkroom.

With the portrait finished at last, Jack slipped quietly into the room where "noted spiritualist" Madame Xyla had already begun her standard ritual. Jack knew it by heart.

A single chair remained at the oblong table, directly beside the photogenic Mrs. Harris. In the dim lighting, he could no longer see the fetching angles of her face or discern her expression. Her posture, however, was rigid, and when the group was instructed to join hands, she reached for him with reluctance.

The contact between their fingers sent a tingle of pleasure up Jack's arm. Her hands were gloved, of course, encased in a smooth, silky material that glided over his skin. Her grip was firm and her hand fit nicely into his. He tried to concentrate on the feel of it to distract him from the hairy, sweaty hand of the man on his opposite side.

The seance proceeded in the exact fashion of all Madame Xyla's rituals: raps and taps and a board that chose random letters. Madame's manner wasn't dull—at least to anyone who hadn't witnessed her performance a dozen times—but Jack half-dozed in his chair, waiting for it all to end.

He almost didn't notice the seance had concluded until Mrs. Harris released his hand. He opened his eyes just before Madame herself turned up the light, illuminating all the guests around the table. The ladies appeared highly pleased with the evening's entertainment, with the lone exception of the shrewd

Mrs. Harris. Two of the attending gentlemen seemed likewise charmed. The third and final gentleman, a tall, silver-haired man with lines around his mouth that suggested a perpetual scowl, gave a short grunt.

"Quite something, wasn't it, Bardrick?" one of the other men enthused. "Aren't you amazed at the skill with which Madame Xyla coaxed the reluctant spirits to make their presence known?"

"I am not," the earl replied. Jack had never met the man before, but knew him by reputation. Very rich. Very haughty. Beastly to anyone who crossed him. "Nothing I have seen tonight cannot be replicated by sleight-of-hand or magician's tricks. It is nonsense. Just as the claims of hauntings at my estate are nonsense. Foolishness and chicanery."

"You don't believe the ghostly tales regarding Bardrick Castle?" the earl's friend pressed.

"I do not."

"Heard plenty of talk about it in the last month or so. Didn't realize you disapproved."

The earl huffed. "I'd wager five thousand pounds no man or woman alive can prove my castle haunted." His scowl softened. "In fact, why not do that very thing? A competition. I will host a party. A single fortnight. You will come, of course, Madame Xyla, and bring better tricks than tonight's silly board. Prove my house is haunted and the five thousand pounds are yours. I shall recruit others. All the best spiritualists in England. Compete amongst yourselves, or work together to persuade me and split the prize. The choice is yours."

He strode from the room without a "by your leave" or even a polite nod of the head. The remaining guests rushed after him in a frenzy of whispered words. Only Mrs. Harris departed silently, her lips pursed in thought.

Jack closed the front door behind the last of the guests, pondering this new opportunity. What was Bardrick up to, and why? It was difficult to imagine an arrogant sort like him *wanting* to be proven wrong. Or handing over good money.

"Well, I certainly won't agree to that nonsense!" Madame Xyla yanked off her wig, revealing the short blond curls beneath. "I haven't any better tricks. And you were no help tonight. Wasting your time flirting with that girl."

Jack smirked at her. "Lydia, darling, I flirt with all the girls. You know that." He toyed with the spirit board sitting on the table. "You should get some new tricks. We're going to that party."

"Don't be a fool," Lydia scoffed. "Something's not right about Bardrick's offer. I don't like it."

"I *am* suspicious of his motives, but that only means we're going in prepared. We're going to go, and we're going to win."

"You're daft, Weaver. I'll never convince him."

"No. But I will."

She rolled her eyes.

"Don't believe me? I've conned harder marks than Bardrick. That five thousand is as good as mine. Help me out and I'll give you ten percent."

Lydia snorted.

"Fine, fine. The usual twenty. Start researching new tricks. I have photos to print."

"You're crazy, Jack Weaver," she said to his departing back. "Mad as a hatter."

"Rubbish, darling." Jack grinned as he bounded away with a spring in his step. "Trust me. He'll be the dupe of the century."

2
The Emperor

Tess tugged her cloak closed against the bitter wind. No wonder people believed Bardrick Castle haunted. On a gray, drizzly day like today, the stark, rectangular structure rose from the mist like a massive tombstone, weather-beaten and crusted with lichen. She wondered whose name she might find carved upon it when she drew near.

"It's quite ghastly, don't you think, Miss Cochran?" Tess's new acquaintance asked. The young woman leaned over the side of the wagon for a better look. "I do hope we'll see real ghosts." Lady Virginia Farringdon tossed back her hood, exposing her unblemished dark-brown skin to the bite of the air. Her amber eyes sparkled and her lips were tilted up in a delighted grin. How she remained so cheery was beyond Tess's comprehension.

Tess wiped a droplet of rain from her cheek and adjusted her hood. Riding in the uncomfortable, open-topped vehicle had been the cheapest fare from the train station to the castle. Now, though, she wished she'd spent the money to hire a coach. She was bruised, she was damp, and she didn't think she would be warm ever again. Certainly not inside a drafty, stone fortress.

"You believe, don't you, Miss Cochran?" Lady Virginia continued. She had latched onto Tess at the train station and had declared sharing a wagon ride to be "brilliant" and "great fun." Strangely enough, her opinion on the matter hadn't yet changed. Perhaps being cold and damp was a novelty for an aristocrat.

"I'm a skeptic, in fact," Tess answered. "I would never say for certain ghosts aren't real, but I keep my eyes open for tricks. No one should be duped for their faith."

"Mmm. A fair point. Though I do hope we find you some true proof during this visit."

"I'm always open to the truth, Lady Virginia."

"Oh, call me Ginny, please. I just know we're going to be like sisters!"

Sisters? Tess was glad her hood would hide the startled look on her face. "Ginny it is, then." It would be good to have an ally in the castle, she supposed.

"I'm here only for the ghosts, myself," Ginny went on. "Father thinks I might attempt to make a match with Bardrick, but I think he's too old and not at all pleasant. And I am adamant that a woman should choose her own husband, assuming she wishes to marry at all. Besides, would *you* want to live in a place like this?"

The answer was no, Tess soon discovered, but not for the reasons she had originally thought. Rather than housing the cold, dark interior of a structure built for defense, this castle had been fully remodeled in a style that would have suited the court of Louis XVI. The ceilings were painted with airy frescoes. Carved moldings and intricate pilasters decorated every wall. Chandeliers dripped with crystal, illuminating room after room with a thousand shards of light. She'd never seen so much gilding in her life. Who did the earl think he was? King Midas?

Tess accepted a cup of tea and some light refreshments in a parlor the size of a small house. She surveyed the room as she nibbled and sipped. None of the half-dozen other guests present were familiar to her. Everyone was dressed elegantly, their clothing finer and more in fashion than the dress Tess wore. A nervous tremor shivered through her, passing quickly as she took a deep breath to calm herself. Lady Goosebury, the patroness of the school where Tess had studied as a girl, had secured her invitation. It wouldn't be rescinded, even if she were taken for an impoverished husband-hunter.

"No spiritualists here yet," Ginny sighed in disappointment.

"They'll arrive soon enough," Tess assured her. Lord Bardrick and his occult competition had become the talk of London. Tess had read every report she could get her hands on and memorized the list of psychics and spiritual practitioners invited. Mr. Winford, her editor, had been thrilled when Tess announced her intention to attend the event.

"What a story it will be when you expose them all at once!" he'd crowed. "I can see the headline: 'Debunked by the Dozen! Psychical Practitioners Proven Phony Phantoms!'"

Tess thought his headline as absurd as the fraudulent seance she had attended, but he could call the article anything he wanted. She only cared that it was published and she was paid.

"Who do you think will win?" Ginny asked. "That Madame Xyla is popular, but my friend says she isn't as good as Madame La Fleur."

"I really couldn't say. I haven't seen either of them."

Only "Mrs. Harris" has.

And since she'd needed a proper invitation to this party, Tess was here under her own name. For once.

She was confident Bardrick wouldn't recognize her. He'd hardly looked at her that night, and a middle-class widow of no consequence would be beneath his notice. The only person who might give her trouble was Jack Weaver. Even now, a week later, Tess still wasn't certain what to make of him. He was a flirt and a swindler, but his enthusiasm for photography had struck her as genuine. When he'd stepped up to the camera, he'd become focused and serious. Professional.

He would be here. His name wasn't on the list, but where Madame Xyla went, he was sure to follow. Tess had spent the entire seance looking into Madame Xyla's face. It was too much of a coincidence for two unrelated spiritual fraudsters at the same small event to possess blue eyes with a single brown splotch.

"Well, isn't this the cozy gathering?"

The mesmeric voice pulled Tess toward it before she even realized her head was turning.

Speak of the blue-eyed devil.

She was here. Damn.

It didn't often happen that Jack disliked being right. But the presence of the lovely "Mrs. Harris," who now graced his wall of favorite photographs, made his suspicion a certainty. She was an investigator. He would need to be on his guard until he could figure out for whom.

Jack sauntered in her direction. "Why, Mrs. Harris, how delightful to see you are out of mourning!"

She looked radiant today, shrouded in a soft, pastel blue. The dress had a similar style to the mourning gown she'd worn the last time they'd met: conservative and unadorned, but smartly tailored to emphasize the curves of her body. It suited her.

She met his smile with a tight frown. "I'm sorry, do I know you?"

So that's how she wanted to play, was it? He held her gaze for a moment, giving her a slight skeptical arch of his brows. Her eyes narrowed almost imperceptibly.

"My apologies. I mistook you for an acquaintance." Jack turned to the woman sitting next to her. "Lady Virginia." He offered his most charming smile. "Lovely to see you again. Won't you introduce me to your friend?"

Lady Virginia gave him a blank stare. Which was to be expected, since they'd never been introduced. He'd seen her at a previous event, however, and learned her name and face, as was his habit. Already he recognized three-quarters of the people here. His memory was his greatest asset.

"Jack Weaver," he said, as if reminding her. "We met last year. You were dressed in a lovely cream, with little rosettes around the hem."

"Oh! Of course. Uh, Miss Cochran, this is Mr... Weaver. Mr. Weaver, Miss Cochran. We met only today at the train station, but I can already tell she will be a delightful addition to our party."

Jack bowed to Miss Cochran. "Enchanted. I'm always pleased to meet another who shares my keen interest in all things supernatural."

Her smile made his entire body quiver. An achingly sweet veneer over her tart, biting cynicism. Would she kiss the way she smiled? He would simply have to find out. Seduction would be an excellent way to distract her from her investigations.

"I look forward to broadening my knowledge, Mr. Weaver. I'm always searching for the hidden depths beyond what we see at first glance."

"I don't doubt that in the slightest." He took a step back and nodded to both women. "Now you must excuse me, but I have only just arrived and I have yet to greet our host. Until next time."

He had to force his broad smile into some semblance of stoicism. He really oughtn't take so much pleasure in sparring with a woman who could only be a nuisance. She was a complication in his previously straightforward scheme. A complication who met each of his pointed remarks with an equally sharp barb. A woman of wit and determination, with a smile that could slay a man. Devilishly tempting. But not worth losing five thousand quid over.

Jack found Bardrick in the smoking room, alone with a fat cigar. The chair he occupied had a high back and a wide, solid base, upholstered in an intricate red and gold fabric. Matching curtains on the wall behind him flanked it, giving it the appearance of a throne. The lower, less ornate chairs seemed scattered at first glance, but their placement was anything but unintentional. Only Bardrick's seat commanded a position of power. All others were located in open space, or had poor lines of sight. Jack chuckled softly. What an utterly pretentious ass. This would be easier than he'd expected.

"Good afternoon, my lord," Jack said, inclining his head more than was his custom. He remained standing near the doorway, like a servant bearing a message.

"Who the devil are you?" Bardrick barked.

"Jack Weaver, my lord. I'm a photographer by trade, here to document the events and the results of your fascinating contest. I have collaborated with Madame Xyla in the past, but in this instance I am participating only as an objective observer. I wished to inform you that I will be photographing both the party guests and your exquisite residence. With your permission, of course." He nodded once again.

"Looking to sell your photos to the newspapers?"

"Looking to capture an image of an authentic spirit. This house provides ideal conditions."

Bardrick snorted and stubbed out the end of his cigar into an ashtray. "You're fool enough to believe in that nonsense? Those women are nothing more than cheats and stage magicians."

Jack walked toward the earl, moving in at an angle and lowering his voice. "In all honesty, my lord, I must agree with you. I know popular opinion holds that the weak wills of women allow the spirits to better pass through them, but if they are so weak-willed, how do they summon the spirits to begin with? Utter nonsense."

Good thing Lydia wasn't in the room to hear this speech. She'd likely try to smack him, even though she knew every word for the horseshit it was.

"Good. Glad to hear you talking sense." The earl started

for the door and Jack went with him, keeping just behind his shoulder and slouching a bit to make himself appear shorter.

"Spirits are not and never will be attracted to women," Jack said. "I've done a great deal of research, and all the learned scientists agree that what truly attracts ghosts is power. Where do ghosts most often exist? Battlefields. Fortresses. Places of great upheaval, of strength and cunning. Where men take life into their own hands. That's what makes your home so attractive. A rich tradition of powerful men dominating over the land. A castle of stone, hewn from the earth by sweat and muscle. A bounty of well-earned riches. This, my lord, is testament to the might you and your ancestors have wielded." He waved a hand at the ostentatious decor.

Bardrick paused and Jack's heart jolted. This part of every con was both the most thrilling and the most terrifying. The usual questions rang in his head.

Have I gone too far? Have I misjudged my mark? Will it all be over before it begins?

"You do appear to have *some* sense in your head, boy." Bardrick chuckled. "Go ahead and take your photographs. Take as many as you desire. I want everyone to see this castle as you do."

Jack's skin tingled with the giddy rush of triumph. Bardrick might never believe in spirits, but Jack had him right where he wanted him. "I'll make certain of it, my lord. May I photograph you as well?"

"You may. But you must show me the photographs before you sell them. I won't have some amateur making me look bad in the papers."

"I will strive to capture you as perfectly as possible, my lord. And I promise you will see every photo."

"Excellent. Come. It's time I greeted our spiritualist guests. I'm eager to watch them strive to outdo one another."

"Naturally. May the best man win."

Bardrick laughed again, puffing out his chest, pleased with his narcissistic interpretation of Jack's words. "Well said, boy."

Jack smirked at the man's back, slowing and letting him stride away to offer his condescension to his fawning guests.

"Yes," Jack murmured. "It was, rather."

3
The Devil

Evening 1:
- *no occult activities*
- *greetings of guests and spiritualists*
- *gaming and casual conversation*

Observations:
- *Madame Xyla is skilled with a deck of cards*
- *she came out ahead, but only by a small, unobtrusive amount*
- *likely cheating*
- *Madame La Fleur is loud and flashy*
- *did not play cards, but walked the room remarking on everyone*
- *Jack Weaver played cards with Bardrick and other men (could not see outcome, but Bardrick appeared pleased)*
- *other spiritualists mingled only briefly before retiring*
- *attempting to maintain aura of mystery*
- *strange whimpering noise outside my room (animal? human? creaking floorboards? May be one of the noises causing rumors of ghosts.)*

Tess read over her notes from the previous evening, frowning at her messy penmanship. The first night of the party had carried on well into the night, far past her usual bedtime. She'd been tired when she'd jotted down her observations.

This intermingling of guests and spiritualists would help her cause, she suspected. The mediums were accustomed to performing under controlled circumstances. No one observed them outside their working environments. Here, however, much of their time would be spent waiting or watching others. Would the pressure of playing a role all day for two straight weeks begin to wear on them?

Madame Xyla, for one, had no fear of mingling with ordinary folk. She'd smiled and chatted as she'd played cards, her personality as cool and calm as it had been during the seance. Tess had sat near her much of the evening, and was certain she had the skills to have won big. She'd cheated to keep her opponents happy and at ease. Picking up information to use in her act, no doubt.

Tess made a note to try feeding her some false information.

After tucking the notebook deep into the back of her trunk, Tess checked herself over in the mirror and headed out the door. These first few days would be primarily observational. She'd established a routine during her years as a reporter, and it worked well for her.

Learn the people. Learn the habits. Then delve deeper.

Which meant no sneaking. Yet. When people said patience was a virtue, she didn't think this was what they had in mind.

As Tess was locking her door, the sound of another door opening behind her made her jump. She whirled around to see Jack Weaver step out of the room directly across the hall. His brows lifted only for a moment before he smiled seductively.

"It seems we are neighbors, Miss Cochran. How delightful."

"Not particularly."

He shook his head slowly. "I must be mistaken. It almost sounds as if you don't like me."

If he hadn't been a conman and she a reporter, Tess would have laughed. Instead, she made herself scowl. "That's because I don't like liars and cheats, Mr. Weaver."

He crossed the hall in two swift steps, drawing close

enough to whisper. "But *you* are a liar, beautiful. Even your dear, departed Edgar knows it to be true."

Tess's scowl deepened. Her fibs were only in pursuit of truth. A necessary evil. She lifted her hands to push Weaver away. The error didn't register until her fingers came in contact with his chest. A scoundrel he might be, but he was also dangerously handsome. He wielded flashing eyes and slightly tousled hair with the skill of a master swordsman, and bodily contact played right into his hands. Even so slight a touch made her breath quicken and her skin prickle.

Tess jerked back, banging into the door behind her. "Don't touch me," she threatened.

Weaver stepped away, holding up both hands. The universal gesture of spurious innocence. "*You* touched *me*, beautiful." His hands dropped to his sides and his eyebrows twitched. "Feel free to do it again whenever you'd like."

"*Never* is when I'd like."

An impish smile played across his lips. "Are you *sure* you're not lying again?"

"Not lying," Tess shot back. "But perhaps mistaken. I think I would like to touch you again. A nice hard slap across the face."

"I'm wounded, madame," he replied, laughing. "Here's the truth as I see it: you're only saying that because you've been taught to espouse priggish, moralistic claptrap. If you allowed yourself to examine your feelings, you would admit you find me interesting and perhaps even exciting."

Tess defiantly folded her arms across her chest and scowled at him in a way no proper lady would do. "You know nothing about me, Mr. Weaver."

"On the contrary. I know you're smart. I know you work hard. A woman would have to, to have success in your chosen profession. I know you are as cynical as I in your beliefs regarding both the metaphysical and human nature. I know you grew up poor. I know you possess a rebellious streak. I know you crave adventure. And I know you keep yourself strictly disciplined, even as you chafe at the rules confining you."

Add dangerously observant to dangerously handsome.

Tess let her gaze drift up and down his body before giving her own assessment. "Let's discuss you, then. You are shrewd, observant, with an excellent memory, and you think highly of yourself because of this. You ignore rules and customs except where they suit you. You're unsatisfied with your life and think you deserve better. Madame Xyla is your sister."

"Wrong. We're double first cousins. Sisters married brothers. But good on you to make the connection. Few people ever do."

"You each have a brown patch in otherwise blue eyes. A family trait?"

He nodded.

"It's quite pretty, in my opinion. Is it apparent in photographs?"

He cocked his head to one side. "I don't know. I've never photographed myself, and Madame Xyla's advertisement portraits are all from a distance and never directly facing the camera. I shall have to experiment."

The irreverent swindler gave way to the introspective artist and his eyes took on a far-away look. Several seconds passed in silence before he snapped back to the here-and-now.

"But, as you were saying, I'm a scoundrel, and a bloody brilliant one at that. Correct?"

Tess almost laughed. Bother. Much as she hated to admit he was right, she did find him interesting. And exciting.

You are a man of layers, Jack Weaver. I wonder what else you're hiding.

He crooked an elbow, offering his arm. "May I escort you to breakfast, Miss Cochran? We have a full two weeks ahead of us during which we will never lack for food and drink and we needn't spend so much as a penny. I intend to take full advantage."

Tess bit her lip. He'd been poor once, too. Perhaps he'd even gone hungry. Another layer for her to excavate.

She placed her hand on his arm. "Breakfast sounds lovely. Thank you."

***

"Day two: insufferably boring," Tess muttered. She slipped away from the assembled gathering and up the stairs toward her room. Which wasn't difficult, since she'd spent most of the day standing in the background. The quiet wallflower.

House parties, she could now say with confidence, were not for her. Chats about nothing. Boring games. "Hikes" through the gardens at a pace that would have made a slug groan.

And no mediums to be seen until the evening palm reading.

Tess traced the lines on her hand, just as the spiritualist had done. *You will meet a mysterious stranger—dark and handsome.*

Really? A dark and handsome stranger? She could have come up with something better herself. And the follow-up implication that the meeting would bring her love or wealth was equally absurd.

It all made good financial sense. Tess had the look of a poor spinster. A vague suggestion that she would find herself a husband or become independently wealthy covered most of what the average woman in her situation would desire.

"Palm reading conclusion: so ambiguous as to be impossible to debunk."

The door to her room stood open and a chambermaid was stoking the fire for the evening. Tess gave the girl a smile and lowered herself into a chair, letting her mind wander. Sometimes good ideas came to her when she pushed the world aside and stared off into space. Tonight, however, her brain repeatedly called up thoughts of Jack Weaver and his dual personality. Sad, really, when the best part of her day had been bantering with a self-professed scoundrel.

A distant keening made her turn toward the door.

"What was that?"

"Pardon?" The chambermaid rose from her crouch.

Tess listened intently. The sound came again, a distant mewling she couldn't place as either human or animal.

"That cry in the distance. Or was it a moan or a howl? I heard it last night also."

"Oh, that's only Bonaparte."

"Bonaparte. As in Napoleon?"

The girl shrugged. "He's a cat, miss. Sometimes keeps folks up at night. You learn to ignore him."

"A cat. Of course." That made sense. Any good castle would have at least one cat to keep mice away. And cats made all sorts of noises, some of which sounded quite human. A noisy cat could certainly contribute to rumors of hauntings. At last, something good for her notes.

"I've never seen him, myself," the girl continued. "Doesn't like people, they say. The housekeeper swears he only shows himself to the earl and it's been that way since his lordship was a boy."

"Lord Bardrick is in his fifties," Tess protested. "No cat lives so long."

"I only know what they say, miss." The maid curtsied. "He won't bother you none. Good night, miss."

Tess made her notes for the evening, sorry as they were, then began preparing for bed. She undressed slowly, hanging each layer in the wardrobe with care. She didn't have many dresses and couldn't afford to be sloppy with her clothing. Her fingers had just hooked through her corset laces when the noise began again.

Bonaparte the cat. How ridiculous. Her gaze drifted to her door, the curiosity building inside her. Today had been mostly useless. She wasn't tired after rising so late this morning. A quick stroll through the darkened house to investigate the bizarre tale couldn't hurt anything. People loved animal stories, so perhaps she could work the cat into her exposé. She pulled her dressing gown over her underthings, tying the sash snuggly around her waist.

Lamps had been extinguished for the night, and the hall was nearly black. A single candle burned in a sconce by the servants' staircase, presumably to prevent anyone summoned in the night from falling and injuring themselves. Tess let her eyes adjust a few moments before heading in that direction. The kitchens would be a logical place to begin a search for a cat. If she heard the noise again, she could adjust her direction accordingly.

"Miss Cochran. What a surprise to find you out and about so late."

Tess gritted her teeth and exhaled before turning. Mr. Weaver sauntered down the hall toward her. In the shadows she couldn't make out the state of his clothing, but she wouldn't have been surprised to find it rumpled from an illicit rendezvous.

"I assume you knocked on my bedchamber door and received no answer, so you are setting out to find me?" he asked. "Well, here I am. You may ravish me at your leisure."

Tess opened her mouth to retort, then thought better of it and started out on her exploration, refusing to spar with him again. He followed.

"Miss Cochran, are you spying on someone not myself? I'm devastated."

"I'm simply out for a walk. Nothing more."

"A walk through a haunted castle alone in the middle of the night? Nonsense. I knew you craved adventure. You're looking for clues. Who are you? Scotland Yard? A private investigator? A newspaper reporter?" All teasing had vanished from his tone, replaced with suspicion.

Damn. He knew, more or less, what she was about.

"I am no one of importance and I'm merely looking for a cat." Not really a lie.

Weaver made a skeptical huff as they continued down the stairs and into the next dark hall, his long legs easily matching Tess's hurried pace.

"A cat?" Now he sounded curious. Intrigued, even.

"A possibly immortal cat who has a habit of making strange noises and yet never manifests where he might be observed."

"I see. That is both exceedingly interesting and painfully mundane. Here I thought you had come to this gathering in order to expose me."

Exactly. They were enemies, and she needed to keep that foremost in her mind.

"Would you kindly either return to your room or shut up?" she retorted. "I can't hear anything through all your yammering."

Much to her surprise, Weaver stopped talking, and they walked on in complete silence. He maintained a respectable distance from her person and allowed her to lead the way without complaint. Strangely gentlemanlike for someone who made such brazen flirtations. Once again, she was altogether too fascinated by him.

Bonaparte's wails sounded again, somewhere behind them. Tess turned and backtracked, choosing a different corridor. In the darkness she couldn't tell where in the castle they might be, but the lack of opulent decor suggested they had found the working areas of the house.

The cat, if that's what it was, ceased mewling, but the creaks of the old castle carried down the empty corridors, and their footfalls echoed from the stone walls. Tess could understand the ghostly tales. Its remote location, long history, and vast size gave the home a sense of mystery. Ordinary fears of darkness and unexplained noises were the fuel. Tess found it no more intimidating than her London flat. In daylight the labyrinth of halls would become ordinary, even boring.

The Scoundrel's New Con

She almost said as much to Mr. Weaver, but froze with her mouth halfway open at the sound of a strange clank. Weaver stilled behind her, his hand coming down on her shoulder.

"That was no cat," he whispered.

Some sort of unspoken communication passed between them, and they moved as one toward the noise, stepping with care. He hovered just behind her shoulder, close enough for her to feel his presence, but not so close that they would bump together as they walked.

More clanks followed the first, and soon shuffling sounds and the low murmur of voices joined in. Tess wracked her brain for legitimate reasons people might be up at this time of night. Cleaning up after the party? Unlikely. All food and drink had been cleared away before the palm readings. All guests had retired for the evening, unless they were surreptitiously visiting other bedchambers. Lights were out, the kitchens were closed, and preparations for tomorrow would not begin for hours.

Another clank sounded, louder than before and clearer. More of a clink than a clank, she decided. The sound of glass on glass.

"Careful, damn you!" The voice was muffled, but the words distinguishable. Coming from up ahead.

Tess and Weaver tiptoed closer, until the shape of a door emerged from the gloom, slightly illuminated by narrow slices of light that seeped out from the room beyond. Weaver gripped her arm and tugged gently, guiding her toward a nearby staircase. They hurried up several steps, out of sight of the door, but near enough to listen. Fragments of muted conversation reached her ears.

"Do this right…"

"…days to prepare…"

"Don't fuck it up."

After several minutes, the voices fell silent and the door opened. Every muscle in Tess's body clenched, and she braced herself to scramble up the stairs. Her arm brushed against

Weaver's. He twitched at the contact, but a moment later his hand found hers, squeezing with a grip just tight enough to offer comfort. The illicit touch sparked a tingle of excitement throughout her body. She was holding hands with a scoundrel, and she had no intention of berating him for his presumption. Their mysterious discovery had transformed them into a team, peculiar as that was.

Keys jangled and metal scraped as the door was locked tight. No hope of peeking inside after the men departed. Tess listened to the footsteps move past the staircase and down the hall, fading slowly, until the castle once again settled into an uneasy stillness.

"I'd say that's enough for one night," Weaver murmured.

Tess agreed. She didn't pull her hand from his until they had ascended the stairs and made their way back to the living quarters where their bedchambers were located. After so much time in the darkness, the rare candle-lamps now seemed to illuminate huge swaths of space and Tess could see Weaver well enough to read the expression on his face. He appeared puzzled, serious. They stopped in the center of the hall, directly between their two rooms.

"Well, beautiful, how does that figure into your investigations? Are you on the hunt for traitors to the crown? Perhaps passing coded messages through fraudulent mediums?"

"You have an overactive imagination," Tess retorted. "Most likely those men are servants, stealing from the earl. Worth reporting, but hardly of national import. Or perhaps they're just like you: manufacturing fake ghosts in an attempt to cheat their way to five thousand pounds."

"No ghosts, no treasonous plots. What *do* you believe in, Miss Cochran?"

"Common sense."

He grinned. His eyes traveled up and down, taking in her lack of proper attire. She yanked the dressing gown closed where it had slipped to expose her corset.

"Yes, quite sensible to run about in the middle of the night in a state of dishabille. Next time you visit me wearing only your undergarments, I do hope it will be in a location where I can remove them."

Tess rolled her eyes. "Honestly. I can't believe any woman would ever let you within fifty feet of her. You're an utter, unrepentant rake."

Weaver chuckled. "But you're within fifty feet. And you neither slapped me nor ordered me away."

"My mistake. Shall I remedy that now?"

His grin was a perilously beautiful thing. "You don't want to slap me. You like my impertinence."

Tess bit her lip, wanting to deny it. "How could you possibly know that?" she asked instead.

"Because you have to stop yourself from laughing when I tease you. Because you brazenly display naughty drawings you discover in textbooks. Because you let me hold your hand nearly all the way to your bedchamber door.

"You see, beautiful, seduction must be carefully tailored to the individual. I would never woo a delicate lady with blatant propositions. I would give flowery compliments and spout poetry. It sounds appalling, actually, which is why I don't woo delicate ladies. You, though, are anything but delicate. You're bold and tenacious. You like midnight secrets. You like the thrill of the forbidden. You like to flirt with danger. So here I am. Whenever you're ready. Goodnight, Miss Cochran." He bowed to her and turned away to enter his room.

Tess slipped into her own chamber, locking the door behind her. Tonight *had* been a thrill. One she ought never to have experienced. She flexed her fingers, unable to shake the memory of the warmth and electricity of his touch. Enough with cats and thieves and roguish photographers. She had a job to do and a story to write. That needed to be her focus. Tomorrow night she would remain in her own damned— dratted—room.

4

The Hermit

"Damnation."

Jack scattered the photographs on the table, then picked one out, frowned at it, and tossed it back. He plucked a second image from the pile, then a third, shuffling the photos as if at random.

"Something wrong, old chap? No spirits today?"

Jack glanced up at Sir Cyril Montague, the taller and leaner of Bardrick's otherwise indistinguishable, card-playing sycophants. Like his shorter, stouter friend, Lord Haverstock, he possessed a head of gray-streaked hair, with bushy sideburns and a long, thin moustache. Both men used the same tailor and had many of the same mannerisms. The baron and the baronet, constant shadows to their domineering and far wealthier friend.

Sir Cyril twirled his moustache, bending over the table to look at the photographs.

"Something wrong with the camera," Jack replied. "Strange anomalies. Are you a believer, Sir Cyril?"

Jack already knew he was, from their shared card game the other night. Jack had spent two solid hours pretending to miss large chunks of the conversation due to preoccupation with his cards and extensive deliberation before every play. He'd lost the entirety of the six pounds and seven he'd had on his person, but won the trust of all three other men.

Jack's hands still twitched a bit every time he thought of the money. Those six pounds were to have paid his rent for the next three months.

"I am, indeed," Sir Cyril replied. "I'd been looking forward to seeing some of your photographs. I heard you were able to capture several spirits during Madame Xyla's last performance."

"Three. Though only one was especially clear. The atmosphere that evening wasn't as conducive to breaching the veil between realms as I had hoped."

"Hmm. What's this then?" Sir Cyril picked up the photograph Jack had left sitting atop the others. "Looks like a bit of a ghostly something."

"Spot of glare, I'm afraid," Jack sighed. "I don't know what happened. The lighting outside yesterday was ideal."

"Hold up a moment." Sir Cyril began to rearrange the photographs. "Look at this. Your 'spot' is following us. Moving with our party along the wall of the castle. You've got them all jumbled up."

"Well, I'll be damned." Jack pretended to scrutinize the photos. "It *is* a spectral form! I've never seen one appear in broad daylight before. Bloody brilliant of you to catch the pattern and know it for what it was."

Sir Cyril beamed at the praise. "No more than a bit of observation, you know," he replied with perhaps the most transparent false modesty Jack had ever heard.

"Do you realize what this means?"

"Er..." Sir Cyril's bushy gray brows merged into one.

"As I was saying to Lord Bardrick the other day, I've done extensive reading on the appearance of spirits as relates to my photography. All the true experts agree people and places of power draw them most effectively. But to appear outdoors? They're frightfully sensitive to direct sunlight, you know. Which explains why this one manifests as no more than a nebulous orb. But its mere presence shows the majesty of this storied castle. And of course, look at the men the spirit is following."

Sir Cyril pushed his shoulders back and lifted his chin. "As fine a group as I've ever seen, if I do say so."

"Indeed, sir, indeed. Would you care to sit for an indoor portrait? I would love to see what develops under ideal conditions."

"I most certainly would! Perhaps our generous host will lose some of his skepticism when he hears of this." Sir Cyril gathered up several photographs. "I'll share these with Haverstock. He may wish to take a turn in front of the lens as well."

"Splendid."

Jack gathered up the remaining photographs as Sir Cyril hurried off to boast of his "discovery" to his companions. Miss Cochran appeared at the far edge of one image, standing slightly removed from the group of ladies, observing. Wouldn't she be something posed solo on a bright sunny day? Where the light would highlight her features and illuminate the brighter streaks in her auburn hair? She deserved a full-color photograph, like those Louis Ducos du Hauron was experimenting with in France. Jack had read all about it, fantasizing about the day when he would have the resources to try it himself. In real life, he'd never even *seen* a color photograph.

He left the other men behind and wandered off to the dining room, where a casual luncheon had been spread across the buffet. He built himself a towering sandwich, slathered with spicy spreads and piled with sliced meats. The bread was soft and fresh, a far cry from the day-old loaves he was accustomed to. He really needed to eat better, but photography supplies cost a fair penny and most of the rest of his money went to rent on his hellhole of a flat.

Jack had just settled himself in a chair, happily alone with his repast, when Lydia waltzed into the room in full Madame Xyla regalia.

"Your wig's askew." He took a large bite of his sandwich. Heavenly.

Lydia glared down at him and adjusted the abundant brown ringlets. "I despise it. It's hot, it's itchy, and it's heavy.

Fine for a show, but all day, every day? It's insufferable. I'm beginning to hate you for this deranged plan of yours."

Jack shrugged, his mouthful of food a convenient excuse not to reply.

"And I don't know what horseshit you've been feeding the guests here, but everyone is prattling on about spirits and their attraction to men. As if those pompous toffs needed more reason to walk around with their noses in the air. And now the *one* male spiritualist…"

Jack coughed.

"You don't count. You're only a photographer. The one man among us is all but cackling with delight as he sweet-talks them like a Lothario alone with an innocent. And I have no doubt this is all *your* doing."

Jack swallowed hard and set down his sandwich. "It is, and the plan is working to perfection."

"Perfection is useless if it undermines my career," she snarled. "This is my *life*, Jack, in case you've forgotten. I don't have many options, and I can't afford to lose this one."

He looked up into her furious blue eyes and gave her a nod of genuine sympathy. "I haven't forgotten." Madame Xyla was not only the culmination of years of hard work, she was also Lydia's path to security and independence. As a medium, she commanded respect. She earned her own keep, without resorting to selling her body to a factory or a brothel to survive. "I swore to you before, and I'll swear it again, I will never do anything to undermine your career. You'll never be out on the streets again because of me."

Lydia turned away and began gathering up her own lunch. "How many times do I have to tell you, Weaver, that wasn't your—" She broke off abruptly at the creak of a footstep.

Jack turned around to see who had interrupted. Miss Cochran. Naturally. Hoping to catch them in an unguarded moment, no doubt.

"I'm sorry," she said—sincerely, it seemed. She walked

toward the sideboard with the food. "I didn't mean to disrupt your family chat. I'll grab a bite to eat and be on my way."

Lydia scowled at Jack. "Are you telling everyone these days?"

"Oh, please don't blame him, Miss Weaver," Miss Cochran replied. "I discovered it on my own."

Jack touched a finger to his cheekbone just below his right eye. "She's quite observant."

Lydia's artificially darkened eyebrows rose almost imperceptibly, then scrunched together as she regarded him with a disapproving frown. "So, that's how it is."

"What?"

"A girl catches your eye, you tell her everything. Congratulations on falling for your own tactic."

"Lydia—"

"That's a pretty name," Miss Cochran interrupted. She extended a hand. "Hello, Lydia. I'm Tess. Not short for Teresa, definitely not short for Elizabeth. Perhaps we can be friends?"

Tess. The name fit her perfectly. Tess was forthright and independent, with a wisp of gentle femininity winding around her tough core. Tess was an adventuress, strong and sweet and…

And he really needed to get a hold of himself. She was here to expose them, and he needed to concentrate on that. Any seduction was to distract her, not *him*. He wasn't flirting with her simply because she was refreshing and smart and unconventionally beautiful.

Right, Weaver. You just keep telling yourself that.

Lydia shook Tess's hand, though the frown didn't leave her face. "There's a male medium here. Rowland the Magnificent. I'm sure you heard him boasting this morning. I've given him my place for the evening. He used to be a stage magician. Whatever he does, keep an eye on his left hand. That should give you a few tidbits for your story, Tess Cochran of the Weekly Informer."

Tess's eyes widened in surprise, but she quickly composed herself and smiled. "Thank you, Miss Weaver. That will be helpful." She gathered up some food and departed, leaving Jack and his cousin alone once again.

"How did you know which paper she writes for?" he asked, before diving back into his sandwich.

"Yesterday was a bore. I saw her flipping through stacks of old newspapers. When she was done, I picked up the ones she'd shown the most interest in. One had an article written by T. Cochran. Exposing unsanitary conditions in a hospital. She's a do-gooder. Stay away from her, Jack. She's trouble."

"Mmm," he replied, his mouth still full.

"I'm not joking. This whole thing is rotten. We could live off five thousand pounds for the rest of our lives. Why would Bardrick risk giving away so much?"

"Because he's rich enough he wouldn't even notice? Bigger the prize, the more people talk. He loves the attention."

"It still stinks. I can't help feeling as if *we're* being conned. Believe me, someone is going to be ruined at the end of all this, and I don't want it to be me."

"It won't be. I swear it, Lydia. I can do this." If Bardrick had an ulterior motive, Jack would uncover it. Nothing was going to stand between him and that five thousand.

"Fine." She plopped into the chair beside him. "Don't fuck it up."

Weaver slid into the empty seat beside Tess as silently as the ghosts he supposedly photographed. Goosebumps rose on her flesh. The air seemed to hum with energy. And none of it had anything to do with the spiritualist at the front of the room. No, this was far too corporeal.

You did this to yourself, Tess.

A few single empty places remained in the rows closer to the performance. She could have taken any of them, and given herself a better view. Instead, she'd chosen the empty back row. It gave her the chance to slip away at any time, she'd told herself.

"Good evening, Tess," he murmured. On his lips, her name sounded sensual. Illicitly enticing.

"Not photographing any longer?" she whispered.

"It's past sunset. All the candles in this castle would give me nothing more than a blur on the plate."

She looked at him just long enough to give him a sweet smile. "And here I thought that's exactly what you wanted."

"On the contrary." He edged closer, until no more than an inch separated his body from hers. "I prefer a crisp, sharp photograph. One that exposes every detail."

Thank the Lord the entire room was fixated on Rowland and his little pile of burning papers, or they might have noticed Tess combusting in the back row. Her simple dress felt stifling, and she wanted to tear it from her body to cool her heated skin. The thought of Jack Weaver seeing that skin only made her warmer.

Tess bit her lip. Enough was enough. She was tired of him having control of the situation. She was going to show him she could match him jab for jab.

"Oh, I would love to expose you, Jack." Her whispered words were far too breathy, but she pressed on. "I intend to strip you bare for all the world to see."

"My room, midnight." He straightened up in his seat, scooting his chair a respectable distance away.

"Breakfast, ten a.m.," she shot back. The woman sitting in front of her glanced back, wearing a puzzled frown.

Tess turned her concentration to the charlatan in front of the crowd. One-by-one, he collected folded slips of paper from guests who wished to contact their departed friends or family, lighting each paper in the flame of a candle and setting it in a tray to burn. She was sure he had palmed a paper or two in order to read the names on them, but as Lydia had warned, his hands moved swiftly. His winning smile and soothing voice kept most of the attention on his face as he talked. Tess did her best to ignore it.

Once all the papers were burned, he walked back and forth in front of the audience, searching the faces in the crowd. "You, madame." He reached out a hand to a middle-aged woman in an elegant gray dress. An excellent choice. She was an American. Chances were high she had lost a loved one during the war. Tess had noticed her fiddling with a locket earlier. If Rowland had gotten a look at it, he would know just what to say.

"Sit here, please," Rowland instructed, leading her to the chair beside his own. "The spirits are strong tonight," he intoned.

"Yes, that brandy did burn a bit going down," Jack quipped softly.

Tess choked back a laugh. This was the problem with him. He didn't take himself too seriously. Unlike Rowland the Magnificent, who she expected would be livid when she exposed his secrets, Weaver would take it in stride. He would be annoyed, certainly, that she'd ruined his perfectly good scam, but he wouldn't throw a fit or try to take her to court. In fact, she imagined him shaking her hand and congratulating her on a hard-fought victory.

Or perhaps she was letting his handsome face and quick wit deceive her into thinking he had actual good qualities.

"I can feel him hovering," Rowland was saying, his voice slipping into a monotone as he lowered himself into a chair and closed his eyes. "A name is forming. A 'D.' Not David or Daniel but... Duncan."

The woman burst into tears, and a hot rush of anger surged through Tess. That man was one hundred percent a fraud, and he was using a poor, grieving woman for his own gain.

Tess jumped when a hand touched her arm.

"Relax," Weaver murmured. "Sit back."

Tess obeyed, but only because she didn't need the entire

room to discover she was a reporter. Bad enough the Weaver cousins knew.

"You're angry on her behalf," he whispered. "Don't be."

"He's cheating her. I would wager all the coins in my pocket he palmed her paper and read the name."

"He did. But what does it matter? She wants to speak with the spirits. She believes. This will bring her some peace. Don't be sorry for her. Be glad for her."

Her jaw clenched. "But it's all a lie."

"Sometimes a lie is what people need to hear."

"Says the con man." Tess fixed her eyes on Rowland and his performance, refusing to speak to Weaver any longer, even when he said her name in that husky voice.

Satisfied that she'd spoken to her dead husband, the American woman returned to her seat, clutching her locket tightly and smiling a teary smile. Rowland called up a second victim, a man who turned out to have lost his young daughter, and the process repeated itself. When he resumed his seat, Tess vacated hers, slipping past Weaver and ducking from the room. Weaver followed her, as usual, trailing her all the way up to their bedchamber doors.

"Why did you leave early?" he asked, right as she reached to put her key in the lock.

Tess paused but didn't turn around. "I want it known that I routinely slip out and retire to bed early."

"Ah. So in a few days when you decide to ransack the rooms of all the mediums looking for ways to expose them, no one will think anything of your absence."

She spun to face him. "I am not ransacking anyone's rooms, thank you very much. Just what sort of person do you think I am?"

His lips curved into a devilish smile. "The sort of person who thinks it's exciting to go sneaking about, ransacking rooms."

"Well, you're wrong, clearly. What I am is a seeker of truth. You may think lying is a good thing, but I don't."

He crossed his arms over his chest and lounged against the wall. "All I said was sometimes it's what people need to hear. You saw how that woman looked afterward. Rowland's words truly meant something to her. You can't call that a bad thing."

"You're trying to justify your own unscrupulous business."

"Beautiful, I've done plenty of business far worse than pretending to speak for a ghost. I don't need to justify anything. I take photographs and spirits appear in them. You can believe or disbelieve as you like. You can go ahead and try to prove them false. It won't stop people from believing or buying. People benefit from what I offer. This world is not as black and white as you paint it. And I think you know that, deep down."

Tess shook her head, unable to answer him without admitting he was at least partially right.

"Enough arguing," Jack said. "Let's go prowling around the castle again. Maybe we'll stumble upon those thieves of yours. Or maybe you'll change your mind about ransacking rooms."

No rooms would be ransacked tonight, but primarily because she couldn't pick a lock and she had no intention of breaking down doors. Besides, it was far too early for such drastic measures. Finding a way into the rooms of a medium or two would only be a last resort.

"It would be quite easy," Weaver continued. "These keys?" He waved his own. "All much too similar. Using technology from the time this castle was built, practically. Allow me to demonstrate." He walked to her door and slotted his key into her lock, wiggling it. Without warning, he plucked a pin from her hair.

"What are you…"

She didn't bother to finish the obvious question. Jack bent the pin with his teeth, then slid it into the keyhole underneath his key, poked and prodded for a few seconds, and turned the key. The door swung open.

"And there you have it. Some of these rooms I suspect I wouldn't even need the hairpin."

"You… You…"

Opened my door. You can come into my room at any moment.

The thrill of the forbidden coursed through her veins. He could slip in, unseen. Entice her with his flirtatious words. Do all sorts of gloriously wicked things with no one the wiser. Her pulse began to race.

Jack propped one arm up against her door jamb. "Stole your hairpin? Yes. My apologies. I'll purchase you a new one after I've secured the five thousand pound prize. At the moment, I'm afraid I'm rather short on funds."

"You're not winning anything. I'm going to expose you, remember?"

"Ah, yes. My room. Midnight." He leaned closer. "Or do you prefer your room right now?"

The heat of his body was doing intoxicating things to her once again. In the dim light she couldn't see how blue his eyes were, but she could still make out the single dark spot. His lips were slightly parted, ready to kiss her at the slightest indication of interest.

I'm not interested. I'm not. This was about the story. About the truth.

Tess moved closer. "Tell me about the photographs," she whispered. "How do you make them?"

He angled his head towards her. His lips hovered only a breath from hers. Tess's heart pounded in her chest.

"Albumen paper, dipped in a solution of silver nitrate and dried."

She swatted at his arm. She knew that part, obviously. She'd done plenty of reading up on the process of making a photograph before coming here. "The spirits, you cad."

If she'd believed in spirits, she might have thought one was possessing her, as her hand moved from his arm to his chest, seemingly of its own accord. Her fingers clenched on the lapel of his coat.

"Spirits *like* me," he said. His lips grazed her cheek. The slightest turn of her head and they would be kissing. And not a sweet, tender storybook sort of kissing. Surely she was going out of her mind, because she craved it with everything in her.

"They're drawn to me." He lifted a hand and the pad of his thumb swept over her lower lip. Tess trembled. "The way you're drawn to me."

The distant screech of a phantom feline snapped Tess out of her trance. She took a step away from him, into her room, her heart still hammering. "Tomorrow. Breakfast. Ten a.m. You'll tell me all about your photographs."

He stared at her, his pupils dilated, his chest rising and falling with rapid breaths. "Tomorrow. Ten a.m. You'll kiss me."

Tess ducked into the room and shut the door. Exchanging kisses for secrets seemed the most brilliant of ideas at the moment. Which probably made it the worst idea conceivable.

She locked the door. The tendril of hair hanging loose from her coiffure reminded her it didn't matter. She plucked a second hairpin from her hair and turned it over in her hands.

If he can open my lock, I can open his.

His reply formed in her head, as real as if he'd said it himself.

Anytime you want, beautiful.

5

The Empress

THE THEATRICS OF Rowland the Magnificent hadn't been sufficiently grand to keep the houseguests awake until all hours of the night. In fact, it seemed many of them had retired earlier than on previous nights. The breakfast room at quarter to ten bustled like a London market.

"Miss Cochran! Here!" Lady Virginia stood and waved at Tess in an endearingly ungenteel manner. Tess carried her plate of food over to the empty place and accepted a steaming cup of tea from a servant with a fresh pot. "How are you this morning?"

"A bit tired." Tess hadn't slept well. Her mind had raced long into the night, contemplating methods used to defraud innocent believers and fending off thoughts of wild, clandestine kisses. Fortunately, with the massive audience present for her ten a.m. meeting with Jack, she wouldn't be tempted. Or she would be less tempted, at any rate.

"What did you think of the performance last night?" Ginny asked. "I thought the burning papers overly dramatic, and while his spirit manifestations were good, I didn't think the spirits spoke of anything especially interesting. He is a competent medium, but not a spectacular one."

"My observations were similar," Tess replied. "I'm hoping for something more interesting today."

I'm hoping Weaver will show so I can grill him about his methods.

"At the very least we'll see whether a spirit appears in Sir

Cyril's photograph. Before you arrived, he was boasting about how he'll be the first to pose."

"Excellent. I've taken an interest in photography of late. I hope Mr. Weaver will allow me to observe the entire process from start to finish."

"Oh, he will, don't you worry. All you need do is flutter your lashes a bit. He can hardly take his eyes off you."

"What?" Tess knew he'd been watching her surreptitiously. She'd never thought he would be so obvious others would notice. Especially with the way she kept herself in the background.

"You don't need to look so surprised." Ginny laughed. "Even wallflowers have admirers now and then. And you have a classical sort of look about you that I would expect to appeal to an artist."

I have a skeptical sort of look about me that sparks the interest of a con artist.

A con artist who wasn't here, even though ten a.m. was approaching rapidly. Tess had expected him to be on time, intending to make good on his promise to kiss her. Perhaps he'd arrived before she had, seen the crowd, and decided he couldn't possibly kiss her with so many people around.

That didn't seem like him.

"Come, now, Bardrick, you must own there is some truth to it," Sir Cyril said from across the room. "You've seen the evidence with your own eyes. Watch today as he takes my portrait. I'm certain there will be no trickery involved."

A voice interrupted from the doorway. "Mr. Weaver may be a photographer by trade rather than a medium, but his connection to the spirit world is strong." Heads turned to where Madame Xyla—Lydia Weaver—stood, dressed today in somber black, a thin veil obscuring her face. She swished into the room. "He attended a seance of mine recently, and I felt it in him. He lost his parents at a young age. Ties to death as children lead, sometimes, to spiritual abilities. All children are closer to the realms beyond than we are. Their natural innocence opens them to the Other. Children often see what we as adults cannot or will not. It is a rare person who carries that sight with them into adulthood, but I believe Mr. Weaver to be one such person, and that is why the spirits manifest in his photographs. They trust him to present them as they are, in a true and scientific portrait. I hope you will all consider sitting for a photograph during our stay here. Perhaps some of the same spirits who speak with us will show their faces as well."

Murmurs about the photo shoot spread throughout the room as Lydia glided to the buffet to collect her food, part of the crowd but not one of them. A sad sort of look lingered in her eyes, and Tess wondered if she was simply lonely, or if it was all part of her act. Tess nibbled at her breakfast, watching for anything worthy of jotting in her notebook.

Ginny chattered happily about everything spiritual, and before Tess knew it, her plate and teacup were empty. She tugged on the chain around her neck, pulling her small watch out from beneath her bodice. Ten past ten. Where was Jack?

"You seem distracted, Miss Cochran," Ginny commented. "I hope it isn't because of what I said about Mr. Weaver. I notice you keep looking to the doorway as if waiting for someone."

Tess pinched her lips together and said nothing. For someone who acted frivolous and flighty, Lady Virginia was certainly observant. A fellow reporter, perhaps? A lady of rank could easily hide a secret career in journalism under the guise of writing letters.

"He *is* very handsome," Ginny said.

Very handsome and very late. Maybe she'd misread him. Maybe he'd no more intended to meet her this morning than she had intended to visit his room at midnight. She forced a smile.

"That's true," Tess replied. "Like you, however, I haven't come here to chase men. I have better things to do with my life."

"Good for you, Miss Cochran. Make *him* chase *you*. And

don't let him catch you until you're certain he wants you for the free-spirited, independent woman you are."

"Wise words, Lady Virginia." Tess rose from her seat. "Thank you for the excellent company. I think I'll go have a look at where these spirit photos will take place. No eyelash fluttering needed."

Weaver had chosen his temporary studio well. The windows had to be among the largest in the castle, and ample light flooded a room made brighter still by light-colored walls. An array of mirrors and white cloths rested against one wall, to allow him to angle or diffuse the light as desired.

Tess ran her hand along the top of the camera. The cloth cover was off, the box empty of the plate where the image would form in an almost-miraculous fashion. Despite her research, she didn't know if she had learned enough to spot anything suspicious in his process. She moved behind the camera, pretending she was the photographer, preparing to freeze a moment in time.

"You'll find nothing amiss with the camera."

Tess spun around.

"I apologize for my tardiness," Jack continued, walking toward her, his arms full of photographic equipment. "I overslept and had to go immediately to the darkroom to prepare for the photoshoot."

Tess stepped aside to allow him access to the camera. He propped the wooden box containing the photographic plate against the legs of the camera as he set about making adjustments.

"I'd like to observe your process, if you don't mind," Tess said, eyeing the carefully covered plate.

"You'd like to observe my process even if I do mind," he replied, glancing at her just long enough to give her an impish grin.

"From the beginning," she clarified. "I saw nothing of your preparation of the plate."

"Next time," he promised. "I have nothing to hide."

Jack draped the black cloth carefully over the top of the camera, then positioned and adjusted everything until he seemed satisfied. By the time he had finished, Sir Cyril and half-a-dozen others had entered the room. Jack posed his victim in a ridiculous stance reminiscent of a military portrait. All it was missing was a chestful of medals and a feathered hat.

Jack talked as he worked, explaining each step of the process, as if Tess were no more than an interested student. Every step proceeded just as she had read. Adjust the focus. Attach the plate holder. Pull up the dark plate, remove lens cap, then replace after exposure. Remove the plate holder and repair to the darkroom for development.

Tess followed him into the temporary darkroom in the next room over, mumbling some excuse about her fascination with photography. Jack worked skillfully and efficiently, developing the negative with practiced hands. When it was finished, he pulled the red filter from his lamp and held up the plate for her inspection.

"There's Sir Cyril's spirit," he said, indicating a blurred dark section. "It will be clearer in the positive print."

"How did you do it?"

Jack carefully lowered the negative into a bath of poisonous fixative. "Just as you saw. I took a photograph."

"I want to watch the entire process from the very beginning," Tess repeated. "And inspect the camera in greater detail."

He transferred the negative to the final rinse. "Certainly. Again, I apologize for not making our morning appointment. I've been very much looking forward to kissing you. In fact, the mere thought of it kept me up late, which was in turn responsible for my oversleeping. Therefore, you have only yourself to blame that I did not arrive promptly at ten a.m., kiss you thoroughly, and then invite you to observe the preparation of the collodion plate." He stepped closer to her. "I will now make up for it by ensuring this first kiss of ours is an especially good one."

A fist hammered on the darkroom door. "Weaver? Have I got any spirits?"

"A few minutes more," Jack called through gritted teeth. "Impatient lobcock," he muttered.

"Language, Mr. Weaver," Tess teased. "The man is simply eager to see his photo, just as I was. And there's no need to insult him with such untruths. His wife seems a satisfied enough woman."

Much to Tess's delight, Weaver's jaw came temporarily unhinged. "You shouldn't even know such a word, Miss Cochran, much less know its meaning."

"I read. Quite a lot."

His hands caught her waist, dragging her against him. Her breath caught in her throat. Thousands of tiny flames roared to life, heating every inch of her skin.

"And apparently quite… extensively," Jack murmured. Lord, but the man had seductive talents. He could turn any word into an erotic treatise. His lips moved against hers, gently brushing, seeking an invitation.

Tess gave it to him. She grabbed hold of his coat, keeping his body tight to her own, feeling the hard, angular lines of his torso against her curves. She sealed her mouth firmly to his, and when he swept his tongue across the seam of her lips, she opened for him.

This is insanity.

She was foolish. Oh, so terribly foolish, to be kissing a scoundrel in a darkroom while dozens of houseguests waited just beyond the door. And most foolish of all was that she didn't care.

Jack's silver tongue was as talented at kissing as it was at speaking. Tess would have let him go for hours, or days, exploring her, tasting her, coaxing her to do the same to him. He was a wildfire: dangerous, beautiful, unstoppable. She groaned low in her throat, the sound muffled by his questing mouth. Her breasts tightened, the nipples hardening to stiff peaks. A rush of wet arousal flared between her legs.

With a gasp, she pulled away. This could go no further. Had already gone too far. If she lost her reputation, she lost her job and her livelihood.

"Damn," he breathed. "I should be late more often."

Tess's hands lifted to her hair, checking that it hadn't been mussed during the embrace. She smoothed her skirts. "This can't happen again," she whispered. She whirled away and rushed from the room.

"My photograph?" Sir Cyril asked her eagerly.

"Is finished," she replied. "Mr. Weaver is confident a spirit was present, but we shall all see shortly when he brings out the print for final exposure."

She wanted to flee to her room, to splash herself with cool water and take time to calm her overstimulated nerves, but then how to explain her disappearance into the darkroom? Her impulsive behavior had left her only one option to justify her interest in the camera and her frequent conversation with Weaver. From now on, she was an avid student of photography.

Jack appeared momentarily, holding the exposure box where the final positive print of the photograph would appear.

"Thank you for your assistance, Miss Cochran," he said. "Nothing is more gratifying to a photographer than an eager student in the darkroom."

Tess nodded, fighting a blush. She was doomed.

6
Temperance

The clock striking two a.m. was as good an excuse as any for Jack to call it quits. He'd lost five more pounds playing cards tonight. Five pounds he absolutely did not have, but since he didn't intend to ever pay off the debt, he didn't much care. He could win it back, if necessary. None of these men would be able to catch him cheating.

Or he could ask Lydia to win the money for him. She had the best card skills Jack had ever seen, and she'd never once been caught.

Unlike some of us.

A shudder ran through him at the memory of that awful night. He'd made a careless mistake and it had cost them both dearly. The ugly slash across his abdomen was the only visible scar from two years in prison, but he had plenty of others that went unseen.

He pushed away the unpleasant thought. He'd moved on. Abandoned cards and focused on what he was best at: reading people and charming them. He'd done well today. Sir Cyril and Lord Haverstock were hooked. All evening they'd raved about the spirits that had been unable to resist their natural, manly vigor and had contacted them in one way or another. Bardrick listened to it all with gritted teeth and a forced smile, no longer categorically denying the existence of the spiritual. His ego wouldn't let him do otherwise. Surrounded by staunch believers, he wouldn't allow himself to be seen as the one weak-willed man the spirits ignored. Jack couldn't care less whether the man ever truly believed or not, as long as he pretended to for the sake of his all-important image.

"Madame Xyla was much better than that Rowland fellow, don't you think?" Lady Montague asked another woman as Jack passed by on his way to the stairs.

He grinned. Lydia's performance after dinner had been stellar. She would be pleased to know the women were still discussing it hours later. Best of all, Tess Cochran had no evidence of any trickery. She could only guess at Lydia's methods, and she would probably guess incorrectly.

Tess.

This time, his shudder was of pleasure, not pain. All day long he'd been reliving that stupefying kiss. She'd left him standing in the darkroom with a muddled mind and a throbbing cockstand. He'd been forced to splash a bit of his precious distilled water on his face to cool himself. Fortunately, they were both practiced at slipping back into their public facades.

Jack hadn't quite read her correctly. Rather than a prim and proper miss with an underlying longing for adventure, she was a first-class adventurer who had stuffed herself in a prim and proper box. A subtle difference, but an important one. Tess kissed with passionate abandon and read naughty books. She knew and liked that side of herself. But she'd constrained it for reasons unknown to him. God, how frustrated she must be.

He could go to her, urge her to throw caution to the wind and take a scoundrel into her bed. Or his bed. Or whatever convenient portion of the castle caught her fancy. She might do it.

Or she might kick him in the bollocks. He put the odds at about one-to-one.

Damn whomever had put him directly across the hall from her. Especially now that he'd proven right in front of her how pathetic the skeleton keys that locked the rooms were. Either one of them could enter the other's bedchamber at any time.

He would never be able to sleep under these conditions.

The ghost cat, or whatever it was, yowled in the distance. He'd go exploring, the way they had the other night. He'd wander the castle poking into places he wasn't supposed to be until he was so exhausted he wouldn't be able to get up and knock on her door, even if he wanted to. A sensible plan. He'd probably have to sleep past noon to recover, but Haverstock didn't want to do a photoshoot in the morning anyway.

Jack paced the halls, back and forth, up and down, until all voices and footsteps faded away—the remainder of the household tucked into bed for the night. Some of them with a partner, he suspected. Rowland had been eyeing many of the ladies, probably hoping to prove himself "Magnificent" outside his spiritual pursuits. And Tess had been right about Lady Montague. She gave her husband frequent suggestive glances. Sir Cyril was unlikely to be troubled by a flaccid member.

"And I'm bloody alone."

Which was nothing new, honestly. Jack couldn't afford to keep a mistress. Any brothels inexpensive enough to frequent were of questionable cleanliness, and he'd seen more than enough squalor and disease over the course of his lifetime. He was forced to make do with charming his way to short-term, no-attachment liaisons involving no exchange of coinage.

Unless he was the one getting paid. He'd done that several times, though he was never, ever, under any circumstances telling anyone about it. Lydia would be horrified. She'd worked so damn hard to keep herself from doing that very thing. She'd be furious he hadn't come to her for money.

Jack's maudlin wanderings had taken him to the staircase where he'd hidden with Tess the other night, listening to the voices of possible criminals. He snuck down the stairs and over to the door, pulling out his key. Given how simple the locks were, he doubted there were more than five or six different shapes for the entire castle. Maybe tomorrow night he'd wander about testing which other rooms his key opened.

Much to his surprise, the door swung inward when he put a hand to it. He jumped back, startled. A tiny spot of light—so small he hadn't noticed it from outside the room—winked out of existence.

"Who's there?" he demanded brazenly, because why not? He'd already made his presence known. Might as well pretend he had the upper hand. "Show yourself."

"Jack?" The light reappeared, growing larger and brighter as Tess opened her lamp. "What are you doing here?"

He stepped through the door and closed it behind him, making a quick survey of the room. A wine cellar, apparently, with half-a-dozen narrow racks reaching floor to ceiling.

"I expect I'm doing the same thing you're doing here," he replied. "Sneaking."

Trying to avoid lying in bed imagining various wicked things I'd like to be doing to you.

"I'm *investigating*. Making certain those voices we heard weren't building fake ghostly contraptions for use in a seance."

"And?"

"It seems unlikely," she admitted. "It also doesn't appear that bottles are missing or have been tampered with, so the men weren't stealing or drinking the wine. Now I'm looking for any sort of secret passage or compartment where they might have come from or concealed something."

"Ah. So you read gothic novels as well as pornography. Or pornographic gothic novels? That sounds fun. Debauched by a ghost. Trapped in a secret passage with an unknown and extremely nimble-fingered stranger. Lured into the dark woods by a mysterious voice that calls out dirty words."

Tess turned away, holding her lamp close to the wall and running her fingers along the seams between stones. Jack slipped closer. She couldn't fool him. He'd caught the wide smile that had flashed across her face at his jest.

He blew a stream of air at her ear, doing his best imitation of eerie, whistling wind. "Cock," he whispered.

She twitched, but didn't halt her exploration of the wall.

"Quim." He let his hot breath wash over her skin. "Fucking."

"You are a shameless reprobate," she replied.

"I know. I went out sneaking to avoid you, and now look what's happened. Fornication in the wine cellar."

"We're not—"

They both froze at the sound of a boot against the stone floor. Tess snapped her lamp closed, plunging the room into darkness. She seized a fistful of his shirt and hauled him into a corner, crushing their bodies together.

"Not a sound," she hissed.

7

The Star

THIS WAS WHAT SHE GOT for encouraging her editor to give her more interesting stories than the usual society gossip. Trapped in a wine cellar between a cold, abrasive stone wall and a hot, maddeningly alluring swindler. All because she had needed more excitement in her life.

She could have continued on in her career as she had begun, playing the part of a paid companion or impoverished gentry, standing in the corner at parties and noticing more than anyone realized. It had earned her a living.

It had stifled the life out of her.

Now this new, more dangerous journalistic endeavor had left her stifling in an entirely different way.

Her fingers were still clenched on Jack's shirt. Beneath her hand, his heart thumped in a steady rhythm. His chest rose and fell with each warm breath tickling her earlobe. Her body sizzled in anticipation of an encounter that would never happen. Not after that kiss had taught her exactly how dangerous he could be. She would content herself with her books and her fantasies. She had to.

"Did you leave the door unlocked?" a low voice asked.

"Nah," a second man replied. "Must've been one of the staff, fetching wine for all those damned guests. Stupid idea, to have all these people around."

The first man snorted. "They think the castle is haunted."

The door swung open and the men entered the cellar, lighting their way with a single candle. Tess pulled Jack even tighter against herself and prayed the shadowy corner would hide them.

"Could be haunted. You ever seen that animal that's always making noises in the night?"

"Ghost cat. Terrifying." He put a hand to one of the wine racks and pushed. Bottles clinked as the shelf pivoted, a section of the floor falling away beneath it. "Let's go." The two men vanished down the hole, and a moment later, the trapdoor rose, the wine rack sliding smoothly back into place above it. Darkness descended once again.

A long, silent moment passed before Jack stepped away from her. Tess fumbled in the dark, striking a match to relight her lamp. She crouched on the floor near the secret door, noting the outline of the hatch and the barely-visible wheels beneath the rack that allowed it to move easily and quietly. She pushed gently, but it didn't budge.

"Here," Jack whispered, pointing. "There's a catch. He must have pressed in just the right spot to release it."

Tess moved to where the rack touched the wall. "And there must be more to the mechanism, perhaps behind the wall and certainly down below to allow the trapdoor to open and close from either side. I wonder where it leads."

Jack rose to his feet and offered her a hand up. She accepted, but released him the moment she was upright.

"Probably not wise to follow them tonight," he said. "Shall we go through tomorrow and find out?"

"No." Sneaking out to investigate a mystery having nothing to do with exposing spiritualists was foolhardy in the extreme. Still, the potential for a story far more interesting than ghostly scams was too much to resist. She would go, but she would go alone.

Jack opened the door and held it for her as they slipped back into the hall. "I don't believe for an instant you will let this go. An adventure you can justify as a quest for truth? That has Tess Cochran written all over it."

They started up the stairs. "And what of you, Jack Weaver? You're not my investigative partner. All you want is to harass me until I give up my efforts to expose you."

"Actually, I want to tease you until you allow me to seduce you. Can't I be one of your adventures, Tess? Don't you want to delve deep and strip me down and discover the real man lurking beneath this clothing? Although I must warn you to take care with how you proceed, because I paid good money for this suit and I don't want it damaged."

"Are you ever serious about anything?"

"I'm often serious about a great many things. The trick is identifying which things those are." He yawned. "Oh, good. I might catch some sleep after all. Goodnight, Miss Cochran, unless you'd like to come to bed with me?"

"I would not, but thank you for asking. I appreciate your occasional honesty."

He laughed, and the sound of genuine pleasure ringing through the empty halls caused an unwelcome flutter in her chest. She hurried to her room and locked herself inside, sinking onto the bed and sighing. She needed to continue her observations of his photographic processes, but these midnight meetings had to end. Tomorrow she would slip down that secret passage. Alone.

"Any questions?"

Tess blinked. She'd been mesmerized by the speed and skill with which Jack prepared his photographic plates. He could pour the collodion and swirl it evenly across the glass without spilling a drop. The stains on his fingers from the silver nitrate were few and small, unlike the giant swaths of black she would no doubt acquire if she tried her hand at it.

He slipped the second plate into the silver nitrate bath. "Would you like to try? I have three plate holders and I can usually have all three exposed and developed before the plate dries too much. Don't take too long to decide, though."

Tess nodded. "I'd like that." She'd seen nothing unusual in his preparations, but his quick hands and obvious competence distracted her from her search for chicanery. Perhaps walking through the process herself would reveal something she had missed. And if no spirits appeared in hers, it would be clear proof of his tampering.

She cleaned the glass the way he had done, then poured the collodion into the center, tilting the plate to make the liquid slide across the surface—"flowing the plate," Jack called it. She didn't do nearly as well as he had. Her negative would be blurred and jagged around the edges.

"Not bad," he praised her. "My first time I spilled all over."

Tess dunked her plate into the bath of silver nitrate, admiring the partitioned container that allowed him to sensitize three plates at once. She didn't take her eyes off her plate for the several minutes it soaked. She would do everything herself. No tampering allowed.

She watched him transfer his two plates to the plate holders, then copied him exactly, still not allowing him to touch or manipulate the plate in any fashion. She settled the glass into a plate holder she had examined before they'd even begun, shutting it up tight against any outside exposure.

Lord Haverstock stood waiting before the camera in the next room, having already adopted a silly pose of his own. Jack adjusted the focus and made his two exposures, then allowed Tess to do the same with the glass she had prepared. Nothing about the camera appeared strange to her or in any way different than when she'd looked it over that morning. She copied Jack exactly, checking that the dark plate was securely in place before carrying her newly exposed photo back into the darkroom.

She watched Jack develop his photos before beginning her own. Ghostly forms appeared in both images, much like in the portraits of Sir Cyril taken the day before. How did Jack do it? She hadn't caught him at anything. Given what she knew of his past and Lydia's abilities with cards and mediumistic tricks, it wouldn't be surprising if he could fool her with sleight of hand. She would have to learn what to watch for.

Tess poured the developer over her plate, tilting the glass with care, trying to keep her motions as smooth as Jack's had been. She wasn't entirely successful, but a sense of accomplishment still swelled inside her as the image began to appear.

"I did it!" she marveled. "I—" She gasped. There, on her very own untampered plate, was a faint, wraithlike form.

"Excellent!" Jack grinned at her, his smile pure devilry in the dim red light.

"How did you do it?" Tess demanded.

"I didn't. *You* did. The spirits must be drawn to you, too." He leaned toward her, waggling his eyebrows. "I can understand why."

"How?" she repeated.

"The magic of photography. The power of light. Still a mystery in so many ways."

"Damn you, Jack Weaver, I know you don't believe in spirits!"

He sighed. "People believe what they want to believe. It's not my place to make that decision for them, or for you. But I'd be happy to continue to teach you about photography. You have a good eye, and I thought perhaps you enjoyed the process?"

"I did. Until this trick of yours appeared."

He took the plate from her hands and dunked it in the fixative. "No need for you to handle the deadly chemicals just yet. I'd hate for you to end up one of the ghosts in my photos. Maybe later we can make another photo, taking a bit more time, and I can show you how I stand and hold everything to avoid contact with the chemicals."

His words were light, but she could read the seriousness

in his eyes. She nodded. "I swear I won't touch any of the chemicals until I've learned all the proper safety measures."

Photography wasn't a profession to be taken up carelessly or without proper instruction. How had he stumbled into it? He was skilled and seemed to enjoy it. He was different when he was working, losing much of the devil-may-care attitude that hid whatever parts of himself he didn't want exposed.

Tess couldn't blame him for that. He was far from the only one to wear such a mask. He did, however, have an uncanny ability to poke through cracks in her own armor. She wasn't certain whether she admired that or hated it.

Much too soon, she stood trapped inside a circle of chattering guests, all eager to inspect her mediocre photograph. The ghostly form in her print had the vague outline of a woman, but it was far too hazy to make out further details. Nothing about the photo itself hinted at how Jack had created the illusion.

"Exquisite!" Haverstock declared, beaming at one of Jack's images, where the spirit imprint had appeared far more clearly. Undoubtedly a woman, though her features were indistinct and fully transparent. "I am spellbound! To think, my noble lineage manifests in a connection to the realms beyond! But you cannot doubt it. Look how clearly she appears. My grandmother, without question. I would recognize her anywhere. And full proof that the camera captures reality, for she passed from this world before the invention of this magnificent device."

Heads around the room nodded, echoing the cries of "exquisite" and "magnificent."

Tess looked again at her own photo. The spectral figure could have been anyone's grandmother. Or sister, or cousin. Her head snapped up, her eyes scanning for Lydia Weaver. She stood in the corner, in her Madame Xyla garb, as always, speaking quietly with Madame Le Fleur. Yes. She had the correct body shape to be this ghost woman.

Tess would make another print of the clearest spirit

photograph, exposing it until it was as sharp as possible. Then she could search Jack's collection of photographs for one of Madame Xyla and compare the two. It would offer no firm proof, but it moved her investigation in the right direction. Perhaps tonight, when Jack expected her to investigate the passage in the wine cellar, she could instead sneak into the darkroom.

An odd sense of guilt twisted in her gut. Weaver didn't seem to have much care for most things in the world or for the people he was swindling, but his photography meant something to him. Twice now she'd witnessed his transformation as he worked. Intruding on his cherished space felt a cruel violation.

He's an admitted scoundrel who is fleecing innocent victims and actively attempting to seduce you. He doesn't deserve pity and is probably too hard-hearted to care what you do.

Right. So why didn't that make her feel better?

8
The Fool

JACK SPLAYED HIS CARDS across the table, smiling at the sighs from his opponents. The plan was going well enough he felt no qualms about winning back all of his money and then some. He would look foolish if he lost too often, and tonight was the perfect night to take advantage.

He'd hardly even needed to cheat. Bardrick was distracted and had misplayed twice, Mr. Cooper, an ardent devotee of spiritualism who had joined their table tonight, was a naturally poor player, and Sir Cyril was busy glancing at the ladies' table to flirt with his wife. This house party certainly seemed to bring spice to their relationship. Or perhaps they were that way all the time.

That's the passion I want in a marriage.

Ugh. Jack shoved the ridiculously sentimental thought aside as he dealt out another hand. Ardent love was dangerous. He'd watched the broken-hearted shell of his mother waste away in the year following his father's death. Sometimes he wished they'd gone together, the way Lydia's parents had. Jack honestly wasn't sure which would have hurt more.

"I'm out," Cooper declared after one final, disastrous hand.

Jack gathered up his winnings. Twelve pounds even, and he didn't think Lord Haverstock remembered about the five pounds owed from yesterday. These men tossed around gold sovereigns as if they were farthings.

"A very good evening to you, gentlemen," he said with a

polite incline of his head. "I look forward to playing with you again tomorrow."

"Hunting party tomorrow," Bardrick reminded the group.

"Ah, yes." Jack didn't allow his smile to falter. He'd be staying at the castle. He doubted he could shoot anything unless it was no more than five feet away and standing absolutely still. Worse yet, he couldn't ride a horse. He'd never even had anything to do with horses other than riding behind them in vehicles and dodging their filth when he walked down the street. This was his first foray outside London in his entire life. And he didn't need to demonstrate that fact to the whole party. "I expect I'll be taking advantage of your outing to photograph the castle's interior. I hope to capture some quality images for your publicity photos, my lord."

Bardrick nodded. "Make them good."

"I'll do my best."

Back up in his room, Jack scattered the twelve pounds across multiple hiding places and stripped out of his jacket and waistcoat. He flopped onto his bed, staring up at the ceiling. Too early to go out sneaking. Perhaps he should have stopped by the library and grabbed a book.

Although to be honest, the only thing he wanted to read just now was a smutty gothic novel. The moment he was back in London with his five thousand quid, he was going to the bookseller to see if such a thing existed. Then he would find where Tess lived and offer to read it aloud to her.

"Christ," he swore. This obsession couldn't possibly be healthy. He had clearly been far too long without female companionship.

Jack closed his eyes and reviewed his upcoming photography plans. This party had a long time remaining and his supplies were limited, so he needed to take care to make each photo count. Allowing Tess to take one of Haverstock's shots had played right into his hands, tying the presence of spirits more strongly to the sitter than the photographer.

Eventually Jack gave up on his efforts and headed out to the wine cellar. Even in the dark he knew his way now, but he brought a lamp regardless. When they did climb down the secret passage, he wanted a clear view of what lay beyond.

Jack parked himself on the nearby staircase and waited in the darkness. An eager energy permeated his entire body. He had no notion what they would find beneath the castle, but the mere thought of exploring it with Tess left him tingling with anticipation.

It was delicious. This adventure would provide a perfect opportunity to sneak a few more illicit kisses. If things went well, perhaps they could continue on to further intimacies. The wait both frustrated and thrilled him.

Time drifted by. Anticipation gave way to confusion, then concern. Where was she? He couldn't imagine she would bypass a chance to discover a secret and uncover possible criminal mischief. She couldn't have snuck past him. The clinking of bottles when the trap door opened would have given her away, if nothing else. Had he arrived too late? Or were more sinister forces at work? Perhaps she had taken ill or fallen victim to some accident.

Jack lit his lantern and stood. He would explore the secret passage on his own. If she had somehow entered without his knowledge, perhaps he would catch her up. If not, he would hurry back to reassure himself of her welfare, even if it meant breaking into her room.

An unpleasant sensation twisted in his chest as he slipped into the wine cellar, locking it behind him. What if she was with another man? What if she'd decided that was the sort of adventure she desired tonight, but not with him?

He shouldn't have cared, but he did. He wanted their flirtation to mean something. He liked her, dammit, even if she was bent on destroying his livelihood. Or maybe that was why he liked her. Maybe it was simply the challenge.

That must be it, he lied to himself.

He found the place on the rack that released the catch, and pushed it aside, shining his lamp down into the opening at his feet. Narrow stone steps led down into the darkness. Jack took them slowly, keeping the beam of light ahead of him. A heavy wooden lever tied to a series of gears sat at the bottom of the staircase. He pressed down on it and the trapdoor closed above him. The wine bottles overhead rattled as they settled back into place.

Jack turned in a circle, finding himself closed in on three sides. The only path was a long, empty corridor heading away from the staircase, sloping very slightly downhill. A shudder ran down his spine. The rough stone walls and unending darkness dredged up memories and feelings best left in the past.

You're not trapped here. You're not.

Taking a deep breath to steady himself, he lifted the lamp and set off.

For more than five hundred paces he walked through the endless nothing, finding no rooms or other halls along the dark, dank tunnel. His heart pounded in his chest and he swore he could hear it ringing in his ears, the only sound in the blackness. The heavy stone walls seemed to draw closer the longer he walked. The lantern slipped in his sweaty palm.

Jack walked faster, fighting the rising panic. This wasn't Newgate. He wasn't locked in a filthy cell. There was a way out. There had to be a way out.

A distant whistling sound brought him to a halt. Wind?

Oh, thank God in heaven.

Jack broke into a run, ears perked for the sounds of freedom. Yes, definitely the wind, accompanied by the crash of waves. A whiff of sea air tickled his nose, and soon a cool breeze caressed his skin.

Relief flooded him. The tunnel emerged into a cluster of boulders, arranged—perhaps naturally, perhaps not—in such a way as to hide the entrance from any ships or boats sailing by. He picked his way over and around them before sinking to the sand, breathing hard.

The ocean breeze ruffled his hair, cooling his overheated skin. Jack allowed himself a moment to survey the shoreline as his body at last began to relax.

"Well, I can say I've been to the ocean now. And walked through a smuggler's tunnel."

It was no great surprise the castle had such a thing. This one, however, had never been closed or else had been reopened for modern usage. The key question: what were they smuggling, and why? Was Bardrick involved or was this happening under his nose?

Jack intended to find out. Tess would want to know, too. She would want to walk through the tunnel herself. He would go check on her. Perhaps she'd simply been tired and fallen asleep while waiting for the rest of the household to retire. Lord knew *he* hadn't been sleeping well of late.

He turned away from the water, scrambling over the rocks and boulders up to the gentle, grassy slope that led back to the castle. The doors would all be shut tight for the night, but he could climb in through the window in his temporary studio. He'd opened and closed it a number of times and it didn't appear to lock.

He took a deep breath of fresh air. There would be no going back through the tunnel. A brisk walk under the stars was just the thing. In no time, he'd be at Tess's door, telling her about the smuggling tunnel and perhaps sweet-talking her into another kiss.

Jack located the window he wanted with little difficulty. From outside, it was above his head, but he pushed it open, then hoisted himself up. He sat perched across the sill, one leg inside and one out, when a noise made him freeze.

The door to his darkroom opened. Tess Cochran stepped out, the faint glow of an almost-closed lamp just illuminating her face.

Jack nearly toppled out the window. *What in hell?* After how open he'd been about sharing his work, this was how she treated him? He'd let her make an entire photograph, and she repaid that by poking around, unsupervised, in the dark? His equipment and supplies had cost him a small fortune. He'd sacrificed meals for that equipment. He'd stayed in his shitty flat in order to finance his photography. He'd spent nearly every penny of his savings to buy enough materials to last him this entire trip. How dare she jeopardize that!

And to do it in the dark? With an open flame? That room was full of chemicals that were poisonous, flammable, or both. She could have been killed! She'd promised him to be safe, dammit.

He gripped the window frame so tightly the wood dug into his palms. His chest ached with the betrayal. Which was absurd, because he'd known all along what her goal was. Why should he have expected any different? They weren't lovers. They weren't friends. There was nothing between them except a bit of witty banter and one glorious kiss.

Fuming, he watched her hurry away, as furious with himself as he was with her. Lydia had been right. He'd let himself be flattered and taken in by a pretty face and a sharp mind. Victim of his own damn methods. And now he was never going to taste that luscious mouth again. Never touch the skin beneath those enticingly simple dresses.

"Fuck," he cursed into the darkness.

9

Coins

TESS RUSHED INTO the breakfast room not a moment too soon. She snagged the few remaining bits of food and poured herself a cup of lukewarm tea, taking a seat beside Ginny once again.

"You're late, Miss Cochran." Ginny's eyebrows twitched. "Had a busy night? I do admire a woman who isn't afraid to take charge of her own life."

Tess kept her voice low, her tone even. "My night was eventful, though not in the way you're insinuating. I had a matter that needed looking into."

"You're certain about that? Because Mr. Weaver wandered through here not long ago, looking frazzled and bleary-eyed. He didn't even eat, only filled an enormous mug with coffee and walked out."

"If he's not sleeping well, it's because he's a bounder who's up to no good. Probably seducing one of the other spiritualists."

"He does seem cozy with Madame Xyla."

Tess choked on her tea. Ginny clapped her on the back until she stopped coughing. "I don't think they have that sort of relationship," Tess wheezed. "At all."

Certainly it wasn't unheard of for cousins to become intimate—cousin marriages were common among the insular upper classes—but Jack and Lydia were double first cousins, and acted like siblings from the little Tess had seen of them together. That explained her instant revulsion. It certainly wasn't jealousy.

"They're very… professional."

Stop talking, Tess. You're making it worse.

Ginny chuckled. "Ah, well. No juicy gossip over breakfast today, it seems. Perhaps one of the other ladies will have an interesting tidbit to share when we travel into the village for the day."

"Yes, the village," Tess replied, unable to feign enthusiasm. What a waste of a day. The women sent to shop while the men stomped off to shoot things. Perhaps she could plead a headache and remain at the house with the spiritualists who weren't participating.

"Are you joining us?" Ginny asked. "Or are you staying behind to play photography student? The gentlemen were saying Weaver will be photographing the castle's interior while everyone is out."

Tess smiled. "I think you can guess where I'll be, then."

"Wonderful! And if anything… noteworthy should happen, you must tell me upon my return."

"Nothing will happen."

"Nonsense. He's terribly charming and roguish. It's all frightfully exciting."

"If you like him so much, why don't *you* flirt with him?"

Ginny pinched her lips tightly together, then exhaled. "I can experience scandal only through others. My focus must be the Cause and befriending like-minded women. It is vital I maintain an unblemished reputation. For now."

The lot of a woman. Perfect, docile obedience or ruination. Tess's muscles clenched. Her whole life she'd chafed under the unfair restrictions placed on her sex. She'd already pushed the boundaries with her position as a journalist, but she still felt trapped in so many ways.

"Besides," Ginny continued, "he likes *you*, and you are my friend. I wouldn't interfere with that."

Tess could only shake her head.

Despite Ginny's overactive imagination, Tess truly did

look forward to a day spent photographing the house. She'd enjoyed her brief foray into the world of photography and was excited to learn more, regardless of how much it did or did not help her investigation. She'd made progress in that direction last night. After considerable digging, she'd found a slim folder containing about a dozen photographic prints. Carefully selected, based on the quality of the images and composition. One of them had been of Madame Xyla, veiled and in a dark dress. Tess believed the pose and shape of the figure to be identical to the spirit image in Lord Haverstock's photo. She would be keeping her eyes open for other such "coincidences."

While the rest of the houseguests prepared for their outing, Tess headed for the darkroom, eager to ask Jack what she could help with today. She knocked on the closed door, not wanting to let any light in if he was preparing plates.

The door swung open a moment later. Jack's normally smirking mouth was pulled into a tight frown, and he had dark circles underneath his eyes. He looked so unlike his usual self that Tess had a sudden fear he might have taken ill.

"Go join the rest of the party, Miss Cochran. I have no further need of, or desire for, your assistance." The unnaturally-growled words sounded almost pained.

"Jack, what's wrong? Are you feeling well?"

"I am not, in fact," he snapped. "I'm enraged that I need to waste my time ensuring nothing was harmed during your unauthorized and reckless snooping. Now go away and let me work."

Tess reeled as if she'd been slapped. He knew she'd been there last night? How? She'd been careful to replace everything exactly as she'd found it.

A near-smile touched his lips, though there was no mirth in it. "Surprised to be caught? Or merely annoyed? Not that it matters. I know of your whereabouts last night. Your 'mentorship,' such as it was, is over. Have a good day, Miss Cochran." He spun away and closed the door in her face.

Shocked and angry—both at him and herself—Tess spent several stupefied seconds staring at the solid oak in front of her. Part of her wanted to pound on the door and rail at him. She'd been entirely honest about her intentions to investigate him. He couldn't be surprised by it. He'd even encouraged her to snoop on others, the hypocrite.

She should have expected they would clash like this. They were natural enemies, no matter how they flirted. He lived for lies while she sought truth.

Still, she wished it hadn't happened so soon or made him so cold and harsh. A trip into the village today might have been a more pleasant choice after all.

Tess returned to her bedroom and dozed for a time, trying to catch up on some of the sleep she'd missed due to her nighttime enterprises. She tossed and turned, woken multiple times by unsettling dreams.

Frustrated and determined to make some good of her time alone, she rose and started on her own tour of the castle. Exploring during the day would give her a true picture of the areas that at night caused whispers of ghosts and hauntings. With everyone gone for the day, much of the staff had the day off. No better time to investigate.

And a certain wine cellar was calling to her.

"What the devil is wrong with you?"

Lydia's irritated footsteps echoed off the high ceiling as she stomped through the portrait gallery, but Jack didn't acknowledge her rebuke. He took his time finishing an exposure of the brooding Fifth Earl of Bardrick's portrait before turning around to reply. Lydia was dressed normally today, in a plain blue dress. Her uncovered curls fell to frame her face. It was good to see her looking herself.

"Nothing is wrong with me," he lied, though he really oughtn't have bothered. She could read his lies better than anyone, and any fool could've seen through that particular fabrication.

"Don't be an ass, Weaver. I haven't seen you scowl this much since we were seven and I stole your favorite toy."

Jack turned back to the camera, swapping out the plate holders for a second photo. These life-sized portraits of Bardrick's ancestors were ideal for his purposes.

"Tess Cochran was meddling in my darkroom last night," he admitted.

Lydia's blond brows shot up. "You cannot be surprised by that."

"That room is full of chemicals. She promised she wouldn't do anything dangerous. It wasn't merely a violation of my space. It was foolhardy."

Lydia chortled. "Oh, Jackie. Sweet on a journalist? It's so adorable."

"I'm not sweet on anyone," he snarled, much too defensively. Bloody hell, what was wrong with him? He couldn't seem to keep his emotions under control anymore. Maybe it was the lack of sleep.

"Mmm-hmm."

Jack replaced the lens cap and gathered up the exposed plates, stalking back to the darkroom. "What's that supposed to mean?"

"You know what it means. The girl you like doesn't like you back, and you're angry at the whole world because of it. You're as transparent as the spirits in your photographs."

"Simply because we flirted a bit—"

"A bit? A lot. Jack, everyone knows, and now everyone is going to know you two have had a falling out."

"There's no falling out because there was never an 'us.' I was merely trying to distract her from her absurd investigation."

"Of course. Completely dispassionate seduction. Clearly we've been going about everything all wrong. You should have just seduced some heiress into marrying you, and then we'd be relaxing in a life of luxury. It would have been the perfect plan. Since you so obviously have no emotional involvement in such affairs."

"Fuck you." For the second time that morning, Jack shut the darkroom door in a woman's face. He was an ass.

Fortunately, Lydia had the good sense not to open the door until he'd had plenty of time to develop the negatives. He was examining the finished products and contemplating all the fun photographic tricks he could do with them—Bardrick's great-grandfather would make a brilliant headless photo—when she finally entered.

"Well, no wonder Miss Cochran was snooping," she said. "This door doesn't even lock."

"Wouldn't matter. I already showed her how easy it was to get into any room in the house."

"Of course you did. Because you're sweet on her."

Jack's fingers clenched. "Stop—"

"It doesn't matter. What does matter is that you're going to go find her and you're going to apologize for making an arse of yourself and let her join in on the photography again."

"Are you off your head? She broke a promise and wants to ruin—"

"Shut it," Lydia interrupted. "Everything was going swimmingly, and I'm not going to let you muck it up because your fragile ego was bruised. Go make up with her. Now. Beg her forgiveness, if needed. Your flirtation was the perfect distraction, and it needs to continue. How could you possibly be devoting your time and energy to creating fake spirit photographs when you're so busy romancing the wallflower? The more effort you make to woo Miss Cochran, the more people will trust your photos are exactly what they seem."

"Which they are."

Lydia rolled her eyes. "Go apologize, Weaver. You know you want to."

He did. And would have, if he'd thought it would do any

good. But he couldn't trust Tess. She might smile and forgive his rudeness, but she'd still be working against him. Eventually he'd fall back into the delusion she liked him and be stung again when she showed she didn't. Pushing her away sounded far more sensible.

"I can't force her to like me."

"Kiss her," Lydia suggested. "Rumor has it you're good at that sort of thing. But she's *definitely* not going to like you if you mope about like a lovelorn schoolboy."

Shit. He was going to let Lydia talk him into this.

"I'll do it on one condition."

"What?"

"First you stand in the studio for a handful of poses. I've got guests begging for portraits, and I want all the correct angles and locations."

Damn. If only Tess were a real student, wanting to learn all his techniques and methods in order to help. With two assistants sitting for him, he could set up brilliant shots.

"Shall I gather a few different outfits?" Lydia asked.

"Yes. Including a pair of trousers if you have one."

"Of course I have one. I'm a modern woman. I don't travel anywhere without a pair of trousers."

Jack smiled for the first time that day. "Hurrah for progress."

"Indeed."

Lydia wandered off, leaving him to finish up in the darkroom. He worked slowly, distracted by the thought of a different modern woman in a pair of trousers. He could picture it vividly: a nice, tight pair hugging Tess's lusciously-rounded arse.

Jack groaned. An active imagination had done wonders for him in life, helping him believe grand things were possible even for a homeless orphan in the big city. At times like this, though, he wondered if maybe it was also a curse.

10
The Chariot

A SMUGGLER'S TUNNEL! Tess sat on the beach, watching the ocean waves as she jotted every relevant detail she could think of in her notebook.

- *tunnel is old, but clean = clearly used now*
- *the mechanism to open and close the trapdoor is modern and well-maintained*
- *places on the rocks near the opening have areas scrubbed free of moss or other growth by hands and feet climbing over them*
- *no obvious footprints: tunnel is too clean and sand/gravel of beach blows and shifts too easily*
- *cannot see tunnel opening or people emerging from it from castle*
- *not a long walk from castle, but requires climbing over and around rocks and boulders = not likely to be discovered by fancy ladies and gentlemen*
- *what appears to be a section of a broken, old pier to the north of the opening actually quite sturdy and usable for mooring small craft*
- *broken bits of shipwreck(?) on beach and sticking out of the water nearby – fueling rumors of ghosts? – keeping boats away?*
- *cannot smuggle anything too large due to size of trapdoor*

Tess closed the notebook and pocketed it. She jiggled her leg, needing a release for her nervous energy. A long walk up and down the beach had done little to settle her. Criminal mischief, happening at Bardrick Castle! This could prove a far more interesting and important story than spiritualist swindlers. The desire to throw aside her assignment for this new investigation smoldered inside her, whispering seductive promises of adventure.

Tess Cochran doesn't write gossip. Tess Cochran hunts down criminals.

"And why shouldn't I pursue this?" she said aloud. If she did uncover a story worth telling, it could catapult her career far beyond anything her current job could. Dividing her attention would mean less time devoted to studying the spiritualists, but she already knew about Rowland palming names of deceased relatives and the little levers Madame Le Fleur stepped on to shake tables and produce raps. If she could discover the secret behind Weaver's spirit photographs, that would be enough to titillate readers.

Tess clambered to her feet and started for the castle. From the back, it looked like any English country house, with a massive iron-and-glass conservatory jutting out and wide windows punctuating the brick facade. A trek into the village to learn some local history might be warranted. Tess doubted Bardrick Castle had ever truly been a military fortification, but she suspected it may always have been a smuggler's haven.

The sky had begun to cloud over, so Tess walked quickly back to the castle, entering through the main doors, where a bored footman waved her in with hardly a glance. Her stomach rumbled. She hadn't eaten since breakfast, and it was now nearly four. With few people remaining behind, the next scheduled meal wasn't until dinner, but she could wander down to the kitchens for a pot of tea and a bite to eat, if necessary.

Her determined strides were carrying her in that direction when a voice called out, "Miss Cochran! There you are!"

She spun to face Jack before she could think better of it. *Damn and blast.*

"You forget yourself, Mr. Weaver. We are no longer speaking. Good day." She turned back around and continued on her way, walking even faster.

"Tess!" He jogged to catch up with her. "I've been looking all over for you. Where have you been?"

All the anger and bitterness had vanished from his voice since morning. Tess spared him a quick glance. He looked better, too. Still sleep-deprived, perhaps, but otherwise his usual, handsome self, unmarred by scowls. His hair was mussed, and he'd done away with his coat and tie. Indecently attractive.

Carousing with one of the spiritualists or some chambermaid?

Tess looked resolutely ahead, refusing to engage with him or the conflicted feelings conjured up by his untidy state. "I really don't think it's any of your business where I've been. Weren't you the one who declaimed that our association was 'over' and slammed a door in my face?"

He remained glued to her side, his long legs easily matching her pace. "I know. I was angry. I'm sorry."

"Hmph."

"I overreacted. You scared me, fooling around in there in the dark. It's not safe. And that equipment is vital to me. If anything happens to it, I would be out of a job. You don't want that to happen to me, do you, Miss Cochran? I'd be out on the street. Forced to choose between petty thievery and selling my body to wealthy pleasure-seekers."

Warmth spread across her skin. Even in his apologies he was trying to tease and seduce, damn him. She would not be swayed. She had a job. A legitimate job.

"I did nothing whatsoever to endanger my person or the tools of your trade," she said. "I touched nothing dangerous, as I promised. Perhaps I would be more sympathetic to your plight if your means of income did not revolve around scamming innocent people. You appear to have an aptitude for the art, why can't you simply sell ordinary portraits?"

"Too much competition. Plenty of photography studios have been doing business since I was a babe. Who would choose the young upstart over them? I can only make a living if I offer something others cannot. And that something is the appearance of spirits."

Tess huffed again.

"And I wish to support Lydia. I can use my photos to promote her seances, while she can send clients to me. It's good family business."

"Scammers all around."

Jack stepped in front of her, forcing her to stagger to a halt. "See here," he snapped. His cheeks had reddened and his blue eyes blazed with emotion. "You're a woman making your own way in the world. You should understand how few respectable careers are open to the female sex. Mediums are respected, well-treated, and earn enough to keep themselves fed and housed in a clean, healthy environment. What would you have her do? Break her back in a factory? Sell her favors and risk disease and pregnancy? She worked hard to earn herself a place in a society that doesn't give a damn about most any woman, let alone one who grew up on the wrong side of town."

Tess blew out a slow breath. "I understand. I had to forge my own way as well, and I had the benefit of a proper education. I'm sorry. I don't wish her harm."

This assignment grew worse all the time. Which was the greater evil? Exposing spiritualists and leaving them unemployed, or allowing them to take money under false pretenses? She didn't know.

Jack's posture relaxed, his flushed skin fading to pink. "I love my cousin," he said, his voice now more carefully modulated. "If not for her, I never would have survived after..." He broke off, shaking his head. "Lydia is as intelligent and competent as any man. My mother and my aunt worked alongside their husbands. You, yourself, are vastly superior in brains and sense to all the men at this castle. I'm assuming it's their own inadequacy that makes them refuse women the vote. Any man of real character wouldn't be afraid of a strong woman, he would be proud to stand by her."

Tess gaped at him. "That is a... shockingly radical statement, Mr. Weaver." Oh, she was in trouble now. His love for Lydia—which Tess believed entirely honest and genuine—counterbalanced his remorseless swindling, and his feminist convictions tipped the scales entirely in his favor. How could she dislike him when he espoused many of her dearly held ideals? Worse yet, how could she expose him now?

Jack shrugged. "You didn't really think I only liked the ladies for their other fine attributes, did you?" His penetrating gaze made a steady perusal of Tess's "other fine attributes."

"No," she replied, fighting the urge to throw her arms around him and kiss him again. "You enjoy a battle of wits far too much to only be attracted to the superficial."

He closed the space between them. "Though I must say, beautiful, your superficial is superlative."

Her heart pounded. "How do you do that?"

"Do what?"

"Make me believe what you say."

He grinned. "With you, my lovely truth-seeker, I need only be honest." He grasped her hand and lifted it to his lips, pressing a lengthy kiss to her knuckles.

"Jack." Tess placed her hand against his chest, feeling the steady rhythm of his pulse beneath his shirt. "I don't need to see the superficial you. Show me more of the real you. Not the Jack that can sweet-talk a rock, but the one who gets lost in the art of a photograph and champions women's rights."

He gazed steadily into her eyes, not relinquishing his grip on her hand. "They're both the real me, beautiful. I've merely let you see a bit further down than most."

Tess rocked toward him until their breath co-mingled. "I want to see all the way down."

He dropped her hand and cupped her chin, tilting her head to align their mouths. His lips skimmed across hers. "I know you do, naughty woman. Come and get me."

A violent crack of thunder rattled the windows, startling Tess so much she jumped, extinguishing the spark sizzling between them. She took a step backward.

Jack cursed. Rain cascaded down the windowpanes and hammered on the roof. "We may want to prepare for a sudden influx of drenched houseguests."

Tess nodded. Her throat was dry, her skin flushed. "We should eat something, then, before there is too great a demand on the minimal staff."

"Tess the Sensible, queen of the day so Tess the Reckless can come out at night. Where will you sneak away to tonight, Tess, and may I accompany you?"

She hesitated no more than a moment. It was only right to show him the smuggler's tunnel. They'd learned of the secret entrance together. "Yes, you may."

"Good," he replied.

"I have something to show you," they said together.

They both twitched, then laughed. "The tunnel?" Tess asked.

"I was in it last night. You?"

"Just now, when you were looking for me."

"I should have known. Tonight, then. We'll explore further. My room. Midnight."

Tess bit her lip, then inclined her head. "Midnight."

11
The Moon

"*Tess.*"

Jack drew her closer, moving in for a kiss, but before their lips could meet, she was pulled away, her beautiful face replaced by a dirty, sneering visage with bad teeth and foul breath.

"You know the rules, boy," the thug growled. "Anything of value goes to me."

Jack stretched out toward Tess, but she only slipped further from his reach.

"You wouldn't want to go back on our agreement, now would you?"

Jack clenched his teeth, struggling not to say anything.

"No one touches your sister, and in return you give me the most valuable bits you find. Fair trade."

Blackmail, *Jack wanted to spit*. And she's my *cousin*, not my sister. *He held his tongue, as he always did.*

"I'll be taking that." *The man waved a hand at Tess. Every second carried her further away.*

Jack dug into his pockets, desperate, finding nothing but a handful of pennies. "I have something better!"

The ruffian's laugh chilled Jack down to his bones. "You bear that devil's mark in your eye, boy. Everyone knows you're nothing but a liar." *He turned and walked away. Tess faded into the distance.*

"No!" Jack shot bolt upright, shaking and drenched in sweat.

"I'm sorry. I'll go."

"Tess?" Jack blinked rapidly, trying to throw off the nightmare. He was in his bed, atop the blankets, mostly dressed. He'd fallen asleep. Damn. Was it midnight already?

She took two steps toward him, the glow of her lamp adding to the light of the one beside his bed. "Jack? Are you well? You look a bit pale. I apologize if I bothered you."

"No. I, uh... Bad dream. Must have dozed off." He pushed himself up out of the bed, his head swimming a bit at the change in position.

"I'm very sorry. I'll go. I shouldn't have entered. When you didn't respond to my knocking..."

Jack crossed the room toward her, the happiness caused by her presence chasing away the chill of the dream. His gaze locked on her, awestruck. She had actually come to his room. More remarkably, she'd *entered* his room, entirely of her own accord. She wore her dressing gown again, but it was tied tightly enough he couldn't tell what she was or wasn't wearing beneath it. He hoped she would give him a chance to find out.

"Please don't go," he said. "It was my fault. I shouldn't have lain down. I'm glad to see you. I didn't know whether you would truly keep the appointment or not."

"Only one of us is a liar, Mr. Weaver."

"Oh, is that so, Mrs. Harris? What would poor Edgar say?"

She didn't reply, but made one of her little huffing noises. Jack was beginning to enjoy those exasperated sounds she made when he teased her.

Her ever-curious eyes tracked across his room, taking in the mostly empty space. His suits were carefully stowed in the wardrobe to protect against dirt and damage, and he owned very little else. Her gaze stopped on the pile of provisions on his bedside table. "Why do you have a big pile of fruit and rolls beside your bed?"

"Because this house has a seemingly endless supply of food. It can't hurt to gather up a few extra things. In the event of a catastrophe or the like." He sounded crazy. He probably *was* crazy.

"I gather you've had occasions in your past when you didn't have enough to eat."

"Yes." Jack wasn't about to divulge his entire past to a reporter, but he could hardly deny the obvious. "I admit to a slight paranoia of running out of food entirely."

Right. Six apples, four crusty dinner rolls, and an entire jar of pickles equalled a "slight paranoia." It was more a "major derangement" and a good reason he should never have invited her to his room.

"I'm so sorry. Was Lydia telling the truth then, when she said you were orphaned at a young age? I've been alone since I was ten, but I was at a girls' school so I didn't suffer severe hardship."

"I lost my father when I was eight and my mother a year later. I lived with Lydia's family afterward, until her parents perished in a fire. We were thirteen." He shrugged. "We managed." She didn't need to hear the rest. "What about you? How did you go from fancy girls' school to journalism?"

"It wasn't a fancy school, it was a sensible school for girls without families. We were trained for positions as paid companions, schoolteachers, governesses, and secretaries. As girls in our position usually are."

Telling and not telling. What secrets was she hiding in her past? She hadn't said she was orphaned or referenced her mother and father, alive or dead. "Alone," she had said. Abandoned? Cast out? Removed from a dangerous situation?

"I have difficulty imagining you in any of those professions," he said, hoping to coax a bit more out of her.

"I was a secretary to Lady Mathis for several years, seeing to most of her correspondence. I applied everywhere I could think of for writing jobs until someone took a chance on me. Now I am here. Shall we go out to gather more materials for my stories?"

Jack covered his mouth to hide a yawn. "Let's."

"Unless you're too tired? I can go on my own tonight."

"I'm fine."

She looked skeptical, but she didn't protest when he followed her out the door and locked up. "Shall we try a section of the castle we haven't explored yet?" she suggested. "Since we've both seen the tunnel."

"The far back, perhaps? Near the conservatory?"

Bardrick Castle had been expanded three times in its history, according to the architectural drawings hanging on the wall in the library. Jack had seen most of it during his day-long photo session, but not with Tess, and he hadn't yet made it as far as the most modern addition at the rear of the house. They struck out in that direction, their soft footfalls soon joined by the wails of the perpetually-unseen cat.

"Where are you, Bonaparte?" Tess asked. "I don't believe for a moment you're a ghost."

"Bonaparte?" Jack snorted. "The cat is named Bonaparte? Well, no wonder he doesn't want to show his face around here. Probably worried we'll ship him off to St. Helena."

"The mewling came from over that way."

Jack followed a step behind Tess, trying to suppress his yawns. He'd been up almost the entire night last night, and he hadn't been sleeping well at all here, despite the comfort of the big bed. Gambling all his savings on the five thousand pound prize had put him on edge, and his nightmares had been more frequent than usual. Maybe now that he'd reconciled with Tess, he could convince her to drop her probe into his spirit photos. That would be a burden off his mind.

Bonaparte howled again, closer than Jack had yet heard. Tess put a finger to her lips and continued on, stepping carefully. They had just come within sight of the conservatory's frosted-glass doors, when a small, dark shape streaked past their legs, yowling, only to disappear directly into the wall.

"What the devil?" Jack wondered.

"Where on earth could he have gone?" Tess hurried toward the place where the cat—if that's what it was—had vanished, her lamp fully open in front of her. "Bonaparte!" she called. "Here, kitty!" She knelt down and her lamp wavered. "Oh! Jack, look here!"

Jack dropped to the floor beside her. A tiny swinging door had been set into the wall a few feet from the conservatory door. Tess held it open and pointed her lamp through the opening. Jack craned his neck for a look, but could see no more than a glimpse of greenery. A flash of lightning lit the room for an instant and the steady patter of rain beat down on the glass ceiling.

"The cat must spend much of his time in the conservatory, for such a door to have been fashioned," Tess surmised. "I don't see him through the foliage. Or much of anything, for that matter." She climbed to her feet. "Shall we go inside and take a look?"

"Yes, let's," Jack agreed, standing and dusting himself off. "I've heard some talk of Bardrick having a garden hobby, or at least a plant collecting hobby."

"Not surprising. Showing off rare plants is the sort of mark of status he would enjoy, and his greenhouse looked to be rather enormous from the outside."

Jack withdrew his key from his pocket and reached to unlock the door. His hand froze in midair. "This isn't the usual lock."

"What?" Tess shone her light on the door.

"This lock is vastly superior to anything else I've seen in the castle. Beyond my abilities." He and Tess turned to look at one another.

"Why would he install a special lock on his conservatory?" she mused. "It isn't a matter of theft. Many valuables are out in the open or behind the worthless old locks. The conservatory is modern, so that could potentially account for it, but why lock the conservatory at all when nothing else in the castle is guarded so? I can only think he must be hiding something."

"Stashing smuggled brandy among the potted ferns?" Jack suggested. "Using the room as a studio to take pornographic photographs?"

Tess quirked a single eyebrow in a manner Jack had always wished he were able to do.

"It has ample natural light, it's warm, and provides a nice backdrop," he argued. "It would be a good place for it."

"If Bardrick knows how to take photographs, why would he need you?"

Jack grinned at her. "For the spirits, obviously." He glanced down at the little cat door. "Do you think you can get in that way?"

"I could put an arm through, but what good would that do? I wouldn't be able to reach the door, even if it did unlock from the inside. I wouldn't want to even risk poking my head through, lest I get stuck."

Jack had to laugh. "That *would* be an awkward conversation when you were found there come morning." He yawned again and swayed slightly. He put a hand to the wall to steady himself. "Any other ideas?"

"Yes. We walk you back up to bed. You're falling asleep on your feet. We can come back tomorrow to investigate further. Take a look from the outside, if the rain lets up."

"I'm f—" Another yawn cut the word short. "Fine."

"Bed."

Jack shrugged and complied. It was difficult to resist Tess ordering him into bed, even if she didn't mean it the way he wanted her to. She took his arm and walked him all the way back to his room. She didn't leave when he opened the door, either, seeing him all the way to the bed and standing at his side until he lay down.

"Don't go out sneaking without me," he murmured, the soft bedding already lulling him into a stupor. "'S dangerous."

"I won't. I need to catch up on sleep myself." She covered a yawn. "See?"

Jack reached for her with one hand. "Stay with me." He wasn't sure why he was even asking. He was much too tired to act on his desires. Her presence was so soothing this evening, though, and he didn't want to let that go. More thunder rumbled outside and he used it as an excuse. "I'm terrified of thunderstorms."

Tess shook her head, but she was smiling. "No you're not."

"*You're* terrified of thunderstorms. I will wrap my arms around you and hold you until it passes."

"You're being ridiculous. Goodnight, Jack." She turned toward the door, but froze at the sound of a woman's laughter from out in the hall. Muffled voices and footsteps followed. Tess sat on the edge of the bed. "You win temporarily," she whispered. "I can't be seen leaving your bedchamber."

He scooted close to her and wrapped an arm around her waist. "Give them a few minutes to pass by."

Tess nodded, yawning once more. "No more than a few minutes." She lay down beside him, and he tugged her tight against his chest.

"Don't worry. Too sleepy to seduce you."

"Mmm-hmm."

"Maybe tomorrow."

"Mmm."

Was that a yes? He thought maybe that was a yes. He drifted off to sleep a happy man.

12

The High Priestess

A RAY OF WARM SUNLIGHT across her face tugged Tess gently from the depths of slumber. Her lashes fluttered, her eyes drifting open to greet the morning. Relaxed. Rested. She hadn't slept this well in ages.

She began to stretch, only to discover an arm wrapped tightly around her. Jack! Good Lord.

He hadn't been the only one in need of a long slumber, apparently. How could she have been so foolish as to let herself fall asleep in his arms?

She knew the answer to that. Even now, she wanted to snuggle into his warmth, feel his lean frame pressed against her. Her movements had caused him to stir. How simple it would be to roll toward him and begin their day with a kiss.

Panic intruded on her fantasy. She couldn't be caught here.

Tess scrambled from the bed, rearranging her dressing gown to cover as much as possible. If he looked at her with eyes full of desire, she might lose her resolve.

Jack sat up, looking deliciously disheveled. His cheeks were faintly pink and his eyes bright after a good night's rest, but his brow crinkled with concern.

"Tess? Is something wrong? Oh, God, did I touch you inappropriately? I'm so sorry."

What?

"I was having a lovely dream," he babbled. "I would never have deliberately—"

She held up a hand to stop him. "You did nothing wrong.

You were entirely gentlemanly. But I must leave. Please excuse me." She hurried for the door. *Please, let the hall be empty.*

Tess pressed her ear to the door, listening for any sound at all, but heard nothing except Jack sliding from the bed behind her. She glanced back at him.

Bloody hell.

His erect cock strained the fabric of his trousers, informing her exactly how pleasant his dreams had been. She groped for the door handle, wrenching the door open, needing to get out before she became entirely fixated on what he might do with that generous appendage.

The hall was blessedly empty. She flew across to her room, let herself in and closed the door softly behind her, sagging back against it in relief.

"Lord, Tess, you are out of control," she whispered. She walked to her own bed and flopped onto the coverlet.

Something had to be done.

~⁓

Tess beat Jack down to breakfast, much to her surprise. Even more surprisingly, he took a seat directly beside her, smiling brightly.

"Good morning," he greeted her in an entirely non-flirtatious tone. "I hope you slept well."

"I did, thank you. Did you?"

"More soundly than I have in eons."

"Wonderful!" Ginny exclaimed from Tess's other side. "Tell us, what is your secret?"

Tess nudged Ginny under the table. The last thing she needed was to cause a scandal at breakfast.

"A visit to the conservatory," Jack replied, flashing his charming smile. "The soothing scents of flowers in bloom can ease one's mind and relax the body in preparation for sleep. This was the first night I tried the method and I heartily recommend it."

"The conservatory." Ginny gave Tess a significant look before turning back to Jack. "How interesting. Are there any flowers in particular you recommend?"

"Belladonna," Tess cut in. "And wolfsbane."

"Just so," Jack replied. "You'll sleep like the dead."

Ginny laughed, and heads all around the room turned in their direction. "You two are delightful." She rose from her seat. "Enjoy your breakfast. I look forward to my portrait this afternoon."

"Ginny requested a portrait?" Tess whispered when she had gone.

Jack nodded and swallowed before replying. "Lady Virginia is among a number of guests who will be sitting for photographs today. Will you assist me with the sessions?"

"Yes, I would like that."

They finished their food in silence, the memory of their night-long embrace humming in the air between them like an electric charge. Perhaps there was something to this magnetism business after all. If someone pointed a camera at them this morning, would little sparks appear on the plate?

Tess stared down at her food, determined to conquer this attraction.

As soon as they had finished, Jack escorted her directly to the darkroom. With half-a-dozen clients scheduled for the day, a prompt start was essential.

"I will need to check that I have sufficient quantities of all the necessary chemicals before we begin," Jack said. "I don't want to bring in an exposed photo only to find I'm out of developer, for instance. I'll go through everything with you and explain how best to handle things safely. First, though, I want to look over my photos from yesterday. I abandoned a number of the negatives with Lydia when I set out to look for you and she intended to make the prints for me. It's the only part of the process she likes, which I find baffling. I'm fascinated by every detail."

Tess smiled. "Yes, I can tell."

"Here are a few we took in the portrait gallery. Bardrick's ancestors are—" Jack froze, frowning. He held the photograph closer to the light. "What the hell is that?"

Tess stepped up beside him, scanning the photo. "I see nothing the matter."

"That blur at the bottom." He pointed. "This photo has one, also." He held up a second example.

The blurs were small and indistinct, but otherwise reminiscent of the spirits in his other photographs. Why would that bother him? Had he captured something real, instead of his usual chicanery?

"Why is that so odd?" she asked. "Don't you expect ghostly forms?"

Excitement bubbled inside her. She didn't believe in ghosts, but if something appeared in Jack's photographs that he didn't put there, she might be able to coax him into telling her what it might be and how it had gotten there. The knowledge of how these anomalies formed would go far in expanding her understanding of how photos were made and manipulated.

"These don't resemble ordinary spirits," Jack replied. "The location is unusual. The shape is as well. Something must have interfered with the exposure. It's only on the bottom, fortunately. I can cover that section when I make more prints."

"How do you think it came to be there?"

He only shrugged.

Tess suppressed a sigh. "Are those other photos all of Lydia? And is she wearing trousers?"

"Yes. We took a number of photos yesterday. I will use them to demonstrate poses and arrangements."

Or you will sneak them into other photos as hazy spirits. Tess would be looking for them in today's portraits.

"If you'd like to do something similar, I would be thrilled to shoot your portrait in any sort of costume or pose at all. You are strikingly photogenic."

"Thank you."

"Not everyone is, you know," Jack continued. "But you... The shape of your eyes and the subtle bow of your upper lip, the way the light falls over your cheekbones. I knew you were beautiful the moment I first saw you, but now every time I look I see something more."

Tess took a step backward, not trusting herself to be too near him. "Thank you, Mr. Weaver. You do know how to compliment a woman."

He held her gaze, eyes blazing. "Usually I'm lying."

Tess looked away. "Well, let's get to work then," she said with false cheeriness.

"Yes," Jack sighed. "Let's."

Four hours of photo sessions later, Tess had decided the life of a photographer was not for her. As much as she enjoyed the process both from an artistic and a scientific point of view, repeating it again and again left her exhausted. Jack, on the other hand, appeared full of energy. He could have gone all day, she imagined. He chatted with his clients, posing them and relaxing them as easily as breathing. When they wanted to sit in a way that didn't work for the lighting, he talked them out of it. When they fidgeted too much, he calmed them down. No wonder he'd had success as a swindler. He could sell water to a drowning man.

"Fabulous!" Lady Montague exclaimed, looking at the photo of a friend. "Not as crisp as my Cyril's, but beautifully haunting. What do you think of mine?"

"He seems not entirely able to manifest," the other woman replied. "As if he's reaching for our world but fading too quickly. It's quite... well, 'haunting,' as you said. Do you think he's a ghost who lives here in the castle?"

Tess shook her head. Jack's photos were received with an odd mixture of delight and envy. Everyone longed to have their photo declared the best, the sharpest, the most ethereal, or whatever other designation they could invent. The photographs had become a marker of status. Only the best could conjure spirits, with the best spirits reserved for the most elite of them all.

"What do you think of this nonsense, Madame Xyla?" Tess posed the question quietly, coming to stand beside Lydia in the corner.

"I think my cousin is brilliant," she replied. "He will walk away from this with a stellar reputation. I'm very proud of him."

Tess's stomach lurched. Jack's reputation would be destroyed if she divulged the real secrets behind his spirit photographs. She didn't know how she could do such a thing. Not when she was growing to like him. But the photographs were the hit of the party. Nothing else could take their place in her article.

She needed to get into that conservatory. She needed the other story. Maybe it would be enough and then she could let Jack and Lydia be. The thought of ruining their lives made Tess ill.

"Are you well, Miss Cochran?" Lydia asked. "You've gone pale."

"Tired. I need a break from all these people."

"They are rather tedious. I'll be glad when our time here is over. Please, take a rest. I won't keep you. You'll be coming to my tarot reading tonight, however, won't you?"

Tess smiled. "I wouldn't miss it. I can't wait to see what you do with the cards."

"I'm so glad. I'll add your name to the list of participants." She gave Tess a grin and a nod and hurried off.

"Blast," Tess muttered. What had she just walked into?

Jack stepped slightly to his right, giving him a better view of Tess's reaction to the cards spread on the table before her. Most of the crowd standing around him was watching Lydia, but he'd seen her do this so many times he knew exactly how her hands flipped the cards and could imagine the sound of her voice before she spoke.

"You are torn," Lydia declared. "Conflicted. You strive for obedience, but disobedience is in your nature."

A few people chuckled. Tess fidgeted with a loose thread on her skirt.

Lydia flipped another card. "A quest for truth," she intoned. "But what truth? Do you seek an absolute? The cards say no such truth exists. You must seek your own truth. Your own self. That is what lies before you. You must find your true path, and it is not the path you think you are on."

Tess's mouth pinched into a tight line. Jack almost expected her to leap from her chair and storm off. She clutched the armrests and forced a smile. Lydia continued on, flipping the last few cards and referencing a dark stranger, in a sarcastic nod to the nonsensical palm reading from days ago.

Tess deserted her seat with obvious relief, and Jack slid into the chair across from Lydia, curious what sort of fortune Madame Xyla would predict for him. Tess remained among the observers, her arms crossed over her chest and her expression hard. She hated being the center of attention and she hated being told what to do. And Lydia had told her in front of everyone that she needed to give up her attempt to expose the spiritualists. No one else in the room knew, but Jack doubted that would make Tess any less agitated. He'd soothe her after the readings were done. He had plans for another night in her arms, this time without the immediate plunge into dreamland.

"The Fool," Lydia pronounced, placing a card in front of Jack.

"Well, there's a surprise," he quipped, giving a debonair smile even though what he really wanted was to kick his cousin under the table. The audience laughed.

"It does not mean you are foolish," Lydia replied, losing none of her cool. "You are on a journey, with much to discover, much to learn. The cards will show where you are headed and what choices you must make."

Her hands moved in smooth, natural motions, turning up the cards. She had arranged them with such practiced ease only another card sharp would even guess what she might have done. The image of long-ago Lydia played in Jack's mind, blond pigtails bouncing as she skipped through the gaming house, a deck of cards her constant companion.

She taunted him the entire reading with oblique references to Tess, most implying that he'd be rebuffed at every turn. Lydia's declaration he would be "witness to greatness" was an obvious nod to his photography. One card predicted either an animal or a ghost would follow him home. He hoped it was the latter, because his landlord didn't allow pets.

"May I choose the final card?" he requested.

"If you wish."

Lydia handed Jack the remaining cards, and he shuffled and cut the deck, turning up his desired card.

"The Lovers," she said. Jack could see her smirk beneath her veil. "I suppose you imagine such a card to be interpreted literally. But no. Considered with the cards before, this speaks of an irreversible choice. Nothing rewarding can be gained without sacrifice. Make your decision wisely."

"Thank you, Madame Xyla, that was most informative."

He gave up his place to the next person and went to Tess, whose eyes had already looked to the nearest exit.

"Stay a moment," he whispered.

"I will not. Everyone is looking at us. I can't investigate when so much attention is on me."

"You certainly can. The attention is on *us*. It's a brilliant diversion." His words echoed what Lydia had said to him yesterday. "You're a young lady falling prey to my abundant charms. Certainly not a reporter or anything absurd like that."

"Hmph."

Jack caught her arm. "Stay until Bardrick has his reading."

Her body remained rigid, but she remained where she was. After one more thoroughly unremarkable reading, the earl at last took a seat across from Lydia.

"Tell me, Madame, what do the cards have in store for me?" Bardrick sounded far less skeptical than he had only days before. He sounded almost eager, in fact; but Jack would have wagered this castle that Bardrick remained an unbeliever. What was he playing at?

Lydia placed a card before him. "The Emperor."

Bardrick preened.

"Great things lie before you," Lydia continued, turning up more cards. "But to achieve them, you must walk the path of truth."

She appealed to his ego for a time, telling him through the cards how he had done everything right and had planned well. His title and wealth were well-deserved.

"Your ventures will be successful," Lydia said, "if you believe."

"Believe what?" Bardirck asked. "Believe I will succeed?"

"I know only what the cards tell us. You must believe." She turned up the Wheel of Fortune card. "Choices are coming. If you err, all will be lost."

A bit of uncertainty crept into Bardrick's expression, quickly masked by a frown of displeasure. "I will not err."

"To triumph, you must remember life has both give and take. One wager must be lost for the other to be won."

He stared for a moment at the cards, then rose from the chair. "Thank you, Madame Xyla. I shall leave you to your next guest."

"Watch this," Jack whispered to Tess. He sauntered casually in Bardrick's direction, catching his eye. Bardrick gave him a curt nod. "A powerful reading, my lord."

"It was. A bit cryptic. I'm doubtful."

"They are all cryptic, I'm afraid. From what I've seen, the key to their success is that they cause you to reflect on the current state of your life and what you desire for your future." Jack lowered his voice. "Apparently, if I want the young lady, I must sacrifice something."

"Her maidenhead, mostly likely." Bardrick snickered.

"See? You understand these things. You have some important investments, I imagine. According to your cards, they will bring you wealth, but you must prioritize one venture over another. That's my interpretation. How do you see it?"

"You're smarter than I'd thought when I met you, boy. You do good work."

"Thank you. I try. Your home is as fine a location as I have ever used for my photography."

"Good. Good. I suppose it's about time I sat for a portrait, myself. I have some business to see to, but two days from now I expect you to be ready."

"Certainly, my lord. I would be honored."

"I will want a dozen photos made. Privately, so I might inspect them and choose the best. I trust you will destroy any of which I do not approve."

"Naturally."

"Good. Then we have an arrangement. Two days."

"I will be ready, my lord." Jack bowed and returned to Tess, escorting her toward the door.

"How can you stand to lick that man's boots?" she hissed as they stepped into the hall. "I don't know what you were saying to him, but I could see the bowing and the my-lord-ing."

Jack only grinned. "All I need do is think of five thousand pounds and I'm happy to bow to anyone. Playing the sycophant can be fun when you see how easily they fall into your trap. He's agreed to sit for portraits at last."

"And will spirits appear in them?"

"Obviously. He's the most powerful man in the castle. They will flock to him."

"What rot!"

Jack laughed. "I like your forthright manner, Tess. You

aren't afraid to tell things as you see them. And on that note, what do *you* see in our future? A night of sneaking, perhaps? A second visit to my room? I did turn up The Lovers, you know."

"You cheated to do that."

"So?"

She shook her head. "If the weather holds, we should go out. Hide ourselves in the rocks and watch for boats nearing shore and anyone entering or exiting the tunnel. We can also inspect the conservatory from the outside."

"Mmm," Jack replied. "A good beginning."

13

The Lovers

Tess rapped gently on Jack's door. She didn't dare knock louder and alert anyone in a neighboring room. This was foolish enough as it was. Hopefully tonight he'd be awake and she wouldn't have to break in.

Jack opened the door and looked her up and down. "You're fully dressed. How disappointing." He wasn't fully dressed. How typical. His torso was covered only by a thin, white shirt, partially untucked and with the top two buttons undone. His trousers sat low on his hips, suspenders dangling.

Tess glanced heavenward. "This is an investigation, not a tryst. Let's go."

He didn't even grab a coat, simply walked out the door in his shirtsleeves, hiking up his suspenders and haphazardly shoving the tails of his shirt into his waistband. If he became cold she wouldn't be especially sympathetic.

"Through the tunnel?" he asked. "Or aboveground?"

"Aboveground. In case the tunnel is in use."

"Good." The word carried an unusual measure of relief. Was he claustrophobic? The tunnel wasn't all that small, though it was quite long and somewhat dank.

They descended to the ground floor, and Tess started for the front of the house. Jack stopped her with a hand on her arm.

"It'll be faster to exit nearer the back of the castle. We can hop out a window to maximize stealth."

"Stealth. Because clambering through a window in a dress is stealthy."

"You could take it off," he said, grinning wickedly. "I'll help you."

"Help me out the window or help me take the dress off?"

"Both." He eyed the large blanket she carried tucked under her arm. "Good thinking to bring some bedding. No one wants to get sand up in sensitive areas."

"We are not fucking on the beach," Tess hissed.

"Ooh, what a lovely vocabulary you have. Been reading salacious books recently?"

Yes, she had, but this was neither the time nor the place for such a discussion. In fact, nowhere and at-no-time sounded like just the place for such a discussion.

So why are you here, alone with him in the middle of the night? Again.

Her strides lengthened, carrying her rapidly through the house, seeking an exit not too near either the wine cellar or the conservatory. Jack stuck with her, not speaking. Before she could think to ask whether any of the windows in this part of the house even opened wide enough to admit a person, he'd located one he liked and flung it open.

"I'll lift you through, if you don't mind."

"Er, yes, I sup— suppose!" she squeaked, startled when he swept an arm behind her and lifted her clear off her feet.

Jack swung her toward the window, sliding her through feet first and setting her on the sill without even the slightest tangle in her skirts. "Hop down," he urged.

Tess scooted forward and dropped to the ground, landing gently in the soft grass. Jack was beside her in an instant, closing the window after him to conceal their departure.

"You've done that before. Lifting a woman out the window, I mean."

"Yes. But not to hide lovers from jealous husbands or whatever debauched things you're imagining. Lydia and I used to practice sneaking out as children. You're rather larger than she was back then, but then so am I."

"I wasn't thinking anything debauched," Tess protested. And truly, she hadn't been. She'd been imagining him fleeing an angry man fleeced in a scam, but stopping to help a woman escape some danger. Half criminal, half knight-errant. A ridiculous fantasy, no doubt, but one she couldn't shake.

"Pity," Jack sighed theatrically. "I'd quite like a bit of debauchery."

"Hush. We don't want anyone to know what we're about. Now follow me."

Finding the location of the tunnel was trickier than Tess expected, but eventually the rocky terrain began to appear familiar to her. They chose a secluded spot, close enough to the tunnel to hear anyone coming or going, but where they were unlikely to be stumbled upon. Jack pulled the blanket from under Tess's arm, unfurled it, and spread it across the ground as if preparing for a picnic. He sat down, leaning back against the rocky outcropping behind him, and patted the place beside him.

"Here you are. Plenty of room."

Tess sat, taking care not to touch him. "I actually brought the blanket to wrap up with in the event I grew cold."

"Let me know if you do. You can sit on my lap and I'll wrap the excess fabric around us both."

Tess shivered. That was altogether too tempting. Jack caught the tremble and leaned toward her, bringing their shoulders into contact.

"Are you shivering with cold, beautiful? Or with desire? Either way, my lap is available to you."

"We are here to listen for mischief," she reminded him.

"I see no reason we can't make mischief while we wait."

"Of course *you* don't. But I…" What? Had a reputation to maintain? It hardly mattered whether she was sitting primly beside him or in a wild, carnal embrace. If she were caught here, with him, in any fashion, her reputation was gone.

Which made her question, once again, the wisdom of

having set out on this adventure in the first place. She brushed the thought aside. They wouldn't be caught. No one had the first clue they knew of the tunnel or would leave the house together for any reason. His bedchamber was far more dangerous a location, even when she was simply knocking on the door.

"You want to," Jack said, with absolute conviction. "But you hold yourself back. Tell me, beautiful Tess, why do you resist this when other adventures you take to with such aplomb? Is it me? I'm too blond for you, is that it?"

She poked him with her elbow. "You know you're gorgeous. Now stop talking. You make a terrible snoop."

An uneasy silence fell between them. The noises of nature echoed in her ears: wind and waves and the distant calls of night animals. What if nothing happened tonight? How long would they wait here before giving up? This could become a nightly ritual, sitting and watching, with no idea when, if ever, they would learn more. Every night beside him, restraining herself.

Jack shivered. He ought to have worn his coat. Unfortunately, feelings of sympathy did well up, unbidden. Tess climbed into his lap and tucked the blanket securely around them both.

He nuzzled her ear, his tongue flicking out to caress her earlobe. The tiny touch sent an invisible current of electricity racing throughout her entire body.

"Thank you, beautiful," he murmured.

Tess closed her eyes and relaxed into his embrace. Fighting her attraction was exhausting. This would be better. The closeness of his body would comfort and warm her. His kisses would thrill her. They were safe from discovery and had nothing better to do to pass the time. A bit of cuddling wouldn't hurt and perhaps might do something to ease her lust.

Excuses.

Jack captured her earlobe between his lips and sucked. His hands glided up her torso to cup her breasts, teasing them through the layers of fabric.

So what if she was making excuses? Those excuses were plenty good enough. She let her head loll to one side to give him better access.

"Beautiful and delicious," Jack purred. He kissed down the column of her throat, his fingers working the buttons of her bodice.

Too many layers. It would take him ages to get through them, and she wanted his hands on her skin. Why couldn't she have changed into something simpler?

Tess twisted around, wanting to touch him in return. She knelt in front of him, straddling one thigh, her hands grabbing for the buttons of his shirt. Their mouths crashed together, a frantic tangle of lips and tongue. She was starved for this. Too long starved.

Jack made a delightful moaning sound into her mouth and dragged her closer, until his straining cock pressed against her leg. The thrill of her own power washed over her. She wasn't alone in this madness. He was as ravenous as she was, and it would be her pleasure to pleasure him.

She pried his shirt open, caressing a body more slender than she'd realized from seeing him clothed. He was all hard planes and sharp angles, warm to the touch and dusted with pale hairs. She teased his nipples and kissed along his jawline, the scratch of a day's stubble rasping against her lips.

"God, Tess," he moaned.

He had made his way down to her corset, and he popped the busks open one-by-one, teasing her with his patience. Her nipples had tightened to hard peaks and she ached to feel his fingers there, touching her the way she was touching him.

At long last the corset sprung open and he caressed and kneaded her through her shift. Sighs of pleasure sprang from her lips as she kissed along his throat, feeling the rapid beat of his pulse.

More, more, more.

Nothing was enough. Every touch, every taste added

new fire to her lust. She needed release. Needed to watch him finding his. Her hands dropped to the fastenings of his trousers. Jack made an inarticulate gasping noise as she freed his cock, curling her fingers tightly around him.

"Careful, you oaf!"

Tess's entire body went cold. Jack yanked the dark-colored blanket fully around them, pulling it up to cover his pale hair. Her head dropped against his shoulder, her heart pounding, breaths coming in rapid, terrified gasps.

What had she done? She'd forgotten everything in the haze of her desire. If they'd been any more wild, made any more noise…

"Stop fussing," a second voice grumbled.

"If you damage the specimen, the buyer won't take it and his lordship won't pay us. C'mon, boat's waiting."

"Worst scam ever," man number two grumbled.

"Shut your gob. The big payout's coming soon. He said he liked 'em, remember? Asked for more 'rare specimens.' Many as we could 'bring back from abroad.'" He chortled.

"Worst scam ever," his companion repeated.

Tess's breathing began to slow as the men tromped off down the beach, their voices fading. She straightened up, adjusting her clothing as best she could. Her body still burned, but her shame burned brighter. She'd lost sight of her goals, let herself be taken in by the promise of passion. Her head had to rule, and she'd been listening to it all too infrequently.

Jack fastened his trousers, but didn't bother with his shirt, instead reaching to help her do up her buttons. She pulled back out of his reach. Pain flashed in his eyes and he turned away, gathering up the blanket and folding it.

When the smugglers had moved a safe distance away, Tess and Jack crept through the rocks until they found a sightline to the shore. A boat bobbed in the waves just close enough to be seen in the dim moonlight. A small rowboat had come to shore, collecting whatever specimen was in the box the men had brought through the tunnel. Tess and Jack watched the exchange for a few minutes, before scuttling back to their hideout. They'd seen enough. Once the men had retreated back into the tunnel, Tess rose and dusted off her skirts, gathering herself for the trek back to the castle.

"What the hell are they smuggling?" Jack asked softly. "Exotic animals? Maybe Bonaparte is actually a baby tiger."

Tess was in no mood for levity. "I don't know, but I intend to find out. I *must* gain access to that conservatory. If you know a way, whether it's by picking a lock, stealing a key, or whatever you can think of, I want you to let me know. But I think it's safer if we work apart from now on."

"Tess…"

She shook her head, cutting him off. "I'm not here to have fun. I have a *job*. And so do you. Try to focus on that." She lifted her skirts and ran ahead.

For once, he didn't follow.

14

Swords

His work had lost its joy. For two days, Jack had been going through the motions like an automaton, repeating the steps again and again, never to cease until his clockwork ran down at last. It was his own fault, he supposed, for allowing himself to become so bloody obsessed with a woman. A woman who had told him repeatedly that she had priorities and he wasn't among them.

If only she weren't so damned... everything. Smart, beautiful, fierce, funny, stubborn, sweet, passionate—dear God, so passionate—hard-working, audacious. He wanted to smile at her over his breakfast. He wanted to teach her every single trick he'd learned with the camera and see if she could help him discover some new ones. He wanted to hear every detail of her past: friends she had, what her school was like, her favorite journalistic assignments, what books she'd enjoyed. He wanted to hold her all night, warmed by her body and soothed by her presence.

"I think I've fallen in love," he said to the empty darkroom. "When will she help me up and kiss me to make it feel better?"

A heavy thump rattled the door.

"What's that, boy? Something better?"

Jack sighed and gathered up the newest prints to show to Bardrick. At least the lack of Tess's presence had allowed him to manipulate the photos at his leisure. He'd combined techniques, played with exposures and negatives, and made Bardrick's photo series the best spirit photography he'd ever done. One after another, each successive Earl of Bardrick manifested, none with the sharp clarity of a living person, but all recognizable if one compared the photos to their portraits.

Which the eager party-goers had done with gusto, exclaiming how different the spirits appeared from their staid portraits, even while their faces possessed a clear resemblance. Jack ought to have felt smug at how well everything had turned out, but the only approval he wanted was from the one person who wouldn't give it.

"Here you are, my lord. The final two photographs."

Bardrick took the papers and held them up to the light. He jerked, and nearly lost his grip, his jaw going slack. He'd been pleased with everything he'd seen before, but these two were the very best photos Jack had to offer. Bardrick stood in the center of the shot, dressed in his finest clothes, as noble and arrogant as a king, flanked by the ghosts of his mother and father. The poses of the spirits were different in each photo, but both were clear as day. Even the styles of clothing were distinguishable, and true to the era when the previous earl and countess had still been alive.

Surprise gave way to suspicion in Bardrick's expression, but he quickly schooled it into his usual gruff frown. "How did you summon them?" he demanded.

"I didn't. It's always the sitter who calls forth the spirits. The camera is merely the vehicle through which their energy can be made visible."

Seconds ticked by as Bardrick frowned at the photos. "I may yet owe you some money, boy," he said at last.

Jack nodded. Thank God. The plan was still working. Bardrick's bizarre smuggling scheme happening in the background had added a layer of uncertainty. What was he up to? And why would he allow it to continue with a house full of guests?

Jack had no answers, but at least he still had the prize in

his sight. Because if this entire journey earned him nothing but heartbreak, he wasn't sure he'd recover from the blow.

"Weaver," Bardrick barked. "Did you even hear what I said? Get your head out of the clouds, boy. Are you brooding over the girl?" He sniffed. "There are other girls. Prettier ones. Forget the dull, bookish chit and go buy yourself a whore." He tossed Jack a coin.

Jack didn't even look at the money, just stuffed it into his pocket, hiding his clenched fist. He suppressed the desire to rail at Bardrick beneath visions of all the far-away places he and Tess could travel with the five thousand pounds. "Thank you, my lord," he mumbled.

"Never mind that. The photos. In a few days, when I host our final party and all the spiritualists perform their best tricks for the crowd, you will do one final photo. I will summon a spirit. None of this nonsense about whatever spirit wants to wander by, or more visits from ancestors. I will summon a spirit of my own choosing. A secret spirit no one could guess. And when he appears, everyone will see and know me to be the most worthy of men. A few days more, boy, and then you will weave your magic for me."

"I am honored to be a part of it, my lord."

"You should be." Bardrick started off without another word, taking the photographs with him.

"Excuse me, your lordship?" Jack called.

Bardrick paused. "What do you want?"

"When I was photographing the house, the conservatory was locked. I've heard you have a fine collection inside and I was hoping I might gain access for a few photos."

"Who told you I have a collection? Montague? That man never knows what he's speaking of. You can't trust a man fool enough to fall in love with his own wife."

Memories of his parents and his aunt and uncle danced through Jack's mind. Holding hands, hugging, laughing. Their joy had been the very antithesis of foolish. Only the thinnest shred of sanity stopped Jack from telling Bardrick to go to the devil.

"Plants are my hobby," Bardrick continued. "The conservatory is my personal space, where I needn't bother with the whinging and fawning of the masses."

"A wise idea, my lord, to keep such a space. I will strike it from my list of places still in need of attention."

"You do that."

Jack watched Bardrick's departing back, keeping a smile on his face by mentally reciting all the foul names he would have liked to call the man. At least he'd gotten further evidence that Bardrick was involved in the smuggling operation. They needed a way into that conservatory.

Jack wandered in that direction, pretending to survey the house for additional places to photograph. The most obvious way for Bardrick to keep people out was to have a single key on his person at all times. It would mean, however, that he had to give his lackeys access each time they transported a "specimen" in or out. Jack couldn't imagine him tromping out of bed to open and close the door in the dead of night. He also doubted the earl would trust anyone with keys of their own. Which meant a key hidden in an easily accessible location. All Jack needed to do was find it.

The hall by the conservatory was empty and quiet. He paused there, examining the doors in the daylight. The frosted glass had been reinforced with decorative iron work, a lattice of steel leaves and vines twisting and winding their way up the door. Jack would have found it rather pretty except for his suspicion that it was only there as an added security measure.

He stood silently, staring at nothing and contemplating where the hell one could put a key that was both hard for anyone to stumble upon and easy enough to be accessed by the two oafs who used the tunnel. A furry black head poked out of the little cat door.

"Well, hello there." Jack knelt, beckoning to the cat and

pulling half a sandwich out of his coat pocket. His appetite had been poor recently. Stress did that to him. He hoarded more and ate less, as if preparing himself to live off scraps.

He tossed a bite of meat toward the cat, and it slowly crawled through the door. It was smaller than Jack had expected, still a kitten. Its coat was a shiny black, with a white patch near the right ear. The cat sniffed and pawed at the food, then gobbled it up.

"You're certainly no immortal Napoleonic beast," Jack observed. "You're a sweet little thing. Is it really you making all that noise at night?"

In response, the cat let out a horrific yowling noise that made him wince.

"Yes, you've proven your point. Are you telling me you'd like a bit more food?" He bent down, setting another piece of meat an arm's length away.

The cat eyed him with suspicion, but when Jack neither spoke nor moved, it crept closer.

"Good kitty," he murmured. "You can eat the whole sandwich if you'd like."

The cat settled in for its snack. As its little body relaxed, Jack reached out a hand and gave it a gentle rub behind the ears. It leaned into him and he scratched harder. The cat purred contentedly. A short while later, it—*she*, Jack determined after a brief check—lay happily sprawled on her back while he rubbed her belly.

"You definitely don't deserve to be called Bonaparte," he said. "I think I'll call you Phantom. That was you in my photographs, wasn't it? What do you know of the conservatory, my little ghost?"

His gaze flicked in that direction and he froze. Visible through the crack beneath the door was a mechanical catch, exactly like the one above the door in the wine cellar. An ordinary lock and key could certainly release it, but what if Bardrick didn't want to entrust anyone with a key or risk one being found? What if this door could be opened by the same variety of mechanism used for the secret passage?

Jack scrambled to his feet and rushed to the door. Phantom made a mewl of confused displeasure.

"I'll be right with you, girl. First I need to find the way into your home."

Jack methodically worked his way across the door, his hands running over and under the iron vines, feeling for any switch, crack, or loose part. A quarter of the way down, a steel leaf wobbled beneath his fingers. He grasped it and twisted. The lock turned with a satisfying clunk.

He swallowed a triumphant cry and eased the door open, peering inside without entering. A thick wall of greenery ringed the single vast room, blocking any view from outside. And filling the remaining space were flowers. Hundreds, maybe thousands.

Jack shut the door carefully and checked that the lock fell back into place. He bent to pet the cat once more.

"Thank you for your assistance, Phantom. I'll be seeing you again later tonight. I have a young lady you will want to meet. She needs to see this."

15
The Tower

Tess's rehearsed speech detailing why she and Jack needed to maintain distance winked out of existence the moment she caught the gleam of excitement in his eye. A thrill shot through her. She caught herself just short of grabbing him by his coat.

"Something has happened. Did you find the key?"

His smile spread ear to ear. "Better. I found a mechanical locking apparatus, like in the wine cellar."

"You saw inside?"

He nodded.

"What was there?"

"Come see for yourself."

Tess grabbed her dressing gown and rushed from the room, once again throwing all caution to the wind. She shouldn't have answered his knock. She shouldn't have even been awake at this hour. But she'd been doing some reflection these past two days, and she'd come to the conclusion that she needed to accept that she never had been and never would be Tess Cochran, model of obedience and virtue. Blaming Jack for understanding her character was unfair. She still felt it was unwise for them to spend too much time together—especially alone—but she disliked the distance that had grown between them. Bardrick's boring library hadn't soothed her while Jack was doing all his photography without her.

The floor was cold against her bare feet, but she didn't lack for warmth. Jack's nearness had freshened the memories of the other night, heightening her awareness of his body and the reactions it incited in her own. If circumstances were different, perhaps they would be in bed instead of walking to the conservatory. But she was a journalist and he was a fraud, and in a matter of days their association would be over.

Damn. A few days suddenly seemed far too short. She would miss him, ridiculous as that was. She enjoyed their companionable silence when they walked about at night like this. Even the times he became chatty and she needed to hush him made her smile. She liked his brazen flirtation—all the more so because he wasn't ashamed of anything he said and he never treated her as if she would or should be ashamed to hear it.

She moved closer to him, wanting to soak up all she could get of him in the time they had remaining. Clearly, she'd lost all ability to follow her own advice.

They knew the house so well now that the walk to the conservatory was easy and swift. Jack trained his lamp on the door, pointing at a leaf on the twisting ironwork.

"Watch." He grasped the leaf and turned it. The mechanical sound of the lock turning rang through the silence.

Tess's heart leapt with a new burst of excitement. They were in! She could see for herself what mischief Bardrick was up to and know for certain if she could make a story out of it. They slipped inside and closed the door behind them, checking that it latched securely.

Jack swung the lamp in a wide arc, giving Tess a quick overview of the room's contents. She gasped.

Orchids. More orchids than she had ever thought to see in her lifetime. They filled the space, in pots, on tables, clinging to the branches or stems of larger plants. They covered every surface, leaving only a meandering path through the crowd of blooms. The only obvious oddity was that all the flowers were white.

"What a collection," Tess marveled. "Maybe Bardrick is

innocent after all. Maybe those men are stealing from him. It would be difficult to keep track of every single plant in such a large space."

"Maybe." Jack sounded skeptical, but what else could she expect from a man who trusted no one. He closed the lamp enough to make a smaller, more focused beam and handed it to her. "Let's look around more carefully. This is your adventure, so I'll follow you."

Tess picked a direction at random, but had taken no more than two steps before an ear-splitting yowl made her jump so badly the lamp flickered and nearly went out.

"None of that now, girl," Jack murmured. He rushed ahead into the greenery, emerging momentarily with a furry, black bundle in his arms. "I don't have a sandwich for you tonight, but I can give you cuddles." He scratched the cat behind the ears and it purred.

"Bonaparte is a real cat?" Tess gasped. "And you befriended him?"

"Of course she's a real cat," Jack replied. "You didn't really think her a ghost?"

"Of course not, but—"

"And she doesn't want that silly name. I call her Phantom, and she's a darling." He smiled down at the cat, who nuzzled happily into his stroking palm. Lucky girl.

Tess continued to gape stupidly. She'd already thought the world unfair for putting her beside a delectable man she couldn't have. And now this?

Bad enough he was uncommonly handsome. Now he was the most adorable thing she'd ever seen. What would he do next? Coo at babies while assisting ailing grandmothers across a crowded street?

"You're ruining your reputation as a scoundrel," she teased.

"Nonsense. I'm not the violent, angry sort of scoundrel. I'm the charming, lovable sort. The others take your money by force. I take it with a smile. And a kiss if you're especially lucky." He arched his eyebrows. "Or especially beautiful."

Tess turned away before she could descend further into madness. Orchids. They were her focus.

She started down a narrow path, aiming her light at the plants. The further she walked, the more her brow furrowed.

"This collection makes no sense."

"It does appear lacking in variety," Jack agreed, from much too close behind her shoulder.

"He has only three, or maybe four, species of orchid here," Tess said. "I'm not certain whether those and those are the same or not."

"I can't tell, and it doesn't matter. This 'collection' isn't a collection at all, but some sort of growing operation. He's smuggling orchids."

"But why? These can't possibly be worth… Wait." She paused and opened the lamp a bit wider, shining it on a workbench up ahead. "That's odd."

They jogged to the table, examining the specimens resting atop it. Various snips, wires, and other tools sat neatly beside a dozen or so potted orchids that only partially resembled those filling the conservatory. Their flowers encompassed a variety of colors, and the shapes of petals and leaves differed slightly from both one another and the orchids growing around the conservatory.

"He's dyeing the petals and trimming the flowers to make them look different," Jack chuckled. "And people are falling for it?" He shook his head. "Of course they are. Orchid mania is running rampant among the idle rich. He must have dozens, if not hundreds of suckers, eager for a newly discovered variety."

Tess moved on to the next table over, where more plants sat, accompanied by brushes, paints, droppers, jars of dye, and pitchers of brightly colored water. Beyond were the finished products, row after row of nearly-identical orchids with peculiar color combinations and altered shapes.

"I can see how this might be fun to someone who enjoys working with plants," Jack said. "And it's quite brilliant, really."

Tess turned to glare at him, glad for the annoyance distracting her from the fact that he still held a happy, purring kitten. "Brilliant? Of course you would say that. After all, a single plant could potentially be sold for hundreds of pounds. What could be more brilliant than stealing huge amounts of money as swiftly as possible?"

Jack's entire body clenched, his brows narrowing into a furious scowl. "And why should I care whether some rich fool spends his money on a fake orchid or a real one? Either is a fucking waste. That money could feed a child or pay a doctor. It could make a significant difference to a person barely scraping by. Excuse me if I will never give a single goddamn who steals money from a frivolous bastard or how."

"I'm sorry," Tess said softly, trying to bring the volume of the conversation down to a safer level. She needed to stop lashing out at him. Yes, he had little regard for laws and rules, and treated truth as if it were a matter of opinion, but he'd already shown himself to have strong convictions and deep compassion. He wasn't her father.

She cringed. "I do understand your reasoning. If my own wastrel father had had greater care for his offspring and less for his profligate lifestyle, perhaps..." What? She'd be tucked away in some country house, married to a man who could "provide for her," bored out of her mind, and lusting after passing scoundrels because her intimate life lacked all passion? Perhaps her father had done her a favor after all.

"Yes?" Jack prompted, stepping toward her. "Do go on. Please, tell me everything about yourself. Your parents, your childhood, your schooling, your employment, your hordes of discarded lovers... Or should that be hoards with an 'A'? Do you stash them somewhere for later use? May I jealously challenge them all to mortal combat?"

"It's a horde of *one* and he's a friend, so no you may not."

Jack tucked Phantom into the crook of one arm and reached for Tess with the other. His hand settled on her hip, urging her closer. "Tell me. Tell me everything."

"Jack…"

"Please." The pleading ache in his voice caused a tremor deep inside her. A longing not merely of lust, but of something more. More powerful. More dangerous. Infinitely tempting. "Let me close, Tess. Let me touch the true you."

"The orchids," she gasped as their bodies collided. "My story. The smuggling."

"Damn the orchids," he cursed, his mouth dropping to meet hers.

The clunking of a mechanical lock halted the kiss before their lips touched. Tess doused the lamp, spinning from Jack's arms in a panic. Her hip bumped the workbench, and it trembled, rattling glassware.

"Who's there?" a gruff voice shouted.

Bardrick. Damn it all to hell.

Jack released Phantom, and the little cat screeched in annoyance.

"Noisy beast," Bardrick groused. "Why can't you be quiet and peaceful like your great-grand sire? You're a disgrace to the Bonaparte name."

Tess felt Jack stiffen beside her, and she laid a hand on his arm. Bardrick stomped toward them, grumbling, a glow emerging in the foliage as his lamp neared. Tess grabbed Jack's hand and led him around the back of the workbench, weaving through the maze of orchids as quickly and quietly as possible.

"Never even catch any mice," Bardrick complained. "Only good you've ever done is to make this house seem haunted."

Phantom mewled. Tess and Jack froze and ducked low as heavy footsteps tromped past them.

"Better not have upset my specimens. The first Bonaparte, now there's a cat deserving of an emperor's name."

Tess thanked God for the ranting that covered any rustling

of leaves as she and Jack inched toward the door. The sounds of shuffling tools told her Bardrick had reached the area they had just vacated. No better time to escape.

The door wasn't visible from the work area, but stepping out into the open space set Tess's heart to racing nonetheless. Jack grasped the door handle, turning carefully.

Metal scraped metal, a harsh, rasping wail in the silence. Jack mumbled an oath and shoved the door open.

"Who's there?" Bardrick shouted again.

Tess and Jack bolted, hand-in-hand, tearing down the hall away from the conservatory. They raced up the first set of stairs they came across, then down another hall, winding their way toward their bedchambers. Voices down the corridor halted them in their tracks.

"Let's try the kitchens," Lady Montague giggled. "I'll be a scullery maid and you can be the villain bent on seducing me."

Tess whirled around, her palm sweaty against Jack's, her fingers biting into his flesh. They backpedaled, then ran on, twisting and turning until she'd lost all sense of direction. Jack pulled her up a spiraling stone staircase that could only have been in one of the two round towers from the oldest part of the castle. Their steps slowed as they ascended the steep, narrow stairs. Tess counted.

Fifty steps up, they stopped, sinking together to the floor, their breath coming in rapid gasps. Tess let her head fall against Jack's shoulder. He released her hand and his arm slid around her waist.

When at last she'd caught her breath, she dared to whisper, "Do these stairs lead anywhere?"

"No. Only an empty old attic."

"We should leave. If anyone comes, we'll be trapped here."

His lips brushed her temple. "Bardrick will have given up by now. Besides, we're only lovers meeting in secret."

"So far from our bedchambers?"

"You do enjoy a good adventure."

Tess couldn't suppress a sigh. "Every time I touch you I forget myself and things go awry. I've learned what I needed to learn. Please escort me back to my bedroom."

"Only if you intend to let me inside. Otherwise you can walk there on your own and I'll stay here, pretending my hand is yours."

Wet heat flared between her legs. Damn him. That visual was altogether too erotic.

"It's your choice, of course," Jack continued, "but when else will you have so grand a chance to go cock-fighting with a scoundrel?"

Never.

Away from London, among people unlikely to even remember her name, with his bedchamber only steps away from hers. The answer was unequivocally never.

Tess rolled to face him. "I surrender."

16
Strength

So it was to be the stairs, then, not a bedchamber. Colder, harder, and less comfortable, but Jack didn't mind. The dark, twisty corridor made a perfect location for a grand adventure with his audacious Tess.

"Tell me everything," he said again, pressing a kiss to Tess's throat where her pulse beat out a steady rhythm. "Absolutely everything." He wanted to know her, inside and out, with his mind and his body. To map every curve, discover every secret. He didn't know which he wanted more, only that he wanted all of it. "Tell me a secret you've never told anyone."

"You already know my secrets. I like adventure and I read dirty books."

"Tell me about your one lover. He puzzles me. I would have guessed either none or many."

Tess shook her head. "You don't understand the perils of womanhood. My very first job when I left school was as secretary to a wealthy woman at her estate in Cheshire. I can't tell you the family name, as I swore never to reveal it. Almost immediately upon my arrival, I struck up a friendship with her son."

"Rather an intimate friendship."

"No, we truly were good friends, and still are, but we were deeply attracted to one another. I was seventeen, he a year older. Urges are quite strong during those years, as you know."

Jack's jaw clenched. Actually, he didn't. He'd spent from seventeen to nineteen in prison, ill and half-starved. He'd been too busy trying not to die and avoiding forced buggery to think of much else.

"One thing eventually led to another," Tess continued, "and we had a grand time of it. But we became careless and were caught." She stiffened in Jack's embrace and turned away. "I was dismissed, of course. Ruined. Beyond anything I could have imagined, even though I'd been warned of it my entire life. I couldn't walk down the street without receiving jeers, disgusted looks, or indecent proposals. I had nowhere to go, no job, no prospects, no hope. I was terrified I would end up on the streets. It was…" She shivered and Jack squeezed her gently.

"I understand."

"Charles—my friend—was furious on my behalf. Looking back, I imagine he was half in love with me. Without his mother's knowledge, he wrote me a glowing letter of reference, which led me to the position in London with Lady Mathis. No one in town knew who I was, so the scandal didn't follow me, but I have had to guard my reputation fiercely ever since. I'm not foolish enough to believe I would be so lucky a second time."

"So you must content yourself with naughty stories and fantasies. Fuck. I'm so sorry, Tess. I should never have pressured you. I'll walk you back to your room."

She grabbed hold of his shirt to keep him down. "No, don't. I think we're safe here. Please, let me… Let me be myself for once."

She turned back toward him and he kissed her brow, stroking the auburn hair she'd pulled back into a simple tail.

"I want you always to be yourself," he murmured. "Tell me, beautiful, what does the real you want?"

"She wants your secrets in exchange for hers. A scandalous one. You must have some of those."

Jack's mouth ticked upward in a wry smile. "I started rumors about myself. Fabricated a rakish reputation for a scrawny, penniless young man with no more than a handful of brief conquests."

Tess propped herself up on one arm, her back against the curving stone wall, appraising him in the dim light. "Why? Isn't it better for business if you're charming but not too wild?"

The words he had sworn never to say tumbled out, loosening some long-choked place inside him. "I did it to convince wealthy women it was worthwhile to pay me for my bedroom services."

Tess gaped at him. "You're a… what? A courtesan? Is there a male word for it?"

Jack shrugged. "Close enough. Cons are transient. You either have to change what you're selling or move to a different location, sometimes both. Some people will buy from you over and over, but others will storm angrily back wanting to know why the snake oil was ineffective."

"A reaction which seems entirely justified, in my opinion."

He gave her a little nod. "Duly noted. I was in a lean time in my life. No money, no prospects. I couldn't return to gambling after New—" He broke off with a shudder. He didn't want to speak of his prison days. Especially not here in a dark, stone chamber. He couldn't taint his time with Tess with those memories. "Never mind that. I couldn't gamble. But I needed money. So I sold myself. It didn't bother me, and it earned me enough to eat and to buy my photographic equipment. Please don't tell Lydia."

Tess's hand splayed across his chest, tugging at his shirt where the top two buttons were already undone. The tip of one finger grazed his skin, igniting a rush of heat from head to toe. "Did you enjoy being a courtesan?"

"Usually, yes. Sometimes it was simply work. I like photography better."

She dislodged a button and leaned toward him, her lips skimming along his jawline. "Oh, really?"

His cock throbbed, hungry to feel those soft fingers that so gently teased him elsewhere. "Yes, really," he rasped. "I'd rather have a lover who…" He groaned and hauled Tess against him, desperate for more of her. The stone steps scratched his bare forearm and dug into his side, but he didn't care. "Who likes me," he finished.

"I like you," she breathed.

Their kiss was a frenzied clash of lips and tongues, a desperate merging of mouths that left them both panting. She nipped at his lower lip. He traced hers with his thumb, loving the swollen feel of it. He could have kissed her for hours, drunk on the taste of her, learning every subtle nuance of her eager mouth.

Tess tugged his shirt free from his waistband and he separated from her just long enough to pull it off and cast it aside. She unknotted her dressing gown and shrugged out of it. The nightgown beneath clung to her skin, displaying her plump, round breasts, the taut nipples poking against the thin fabric. Jack cupped them, squeezing and teasing until she sighed with pleasure. That was a sound he could have listened to all night.

"I like you very much," Tess murmured against his lips.

I love you, Jack replied silently.

Her nimble fingers worked his trousers open, shoving them down past his hips before gripping his cock and stroking.

Oh, God, I love you like mad.

He caught her devilish grin before his eyes fluttered closed. "And I would very much like to hear you moan," she whispered.

Her mouth was on his cock before he could even think to reply. His back arched, his hips lifting to beg for more. Great bloody hell and damn. Never in his life had he felt anything so incredible. He'd thought he had a fair amount of experience, despite his exaggerated reputation, but no woman had ever pleasured him this way before. Paying clients tended not to take a great deal of interest in his gratification.

"Tess…" He moaned for her, just as she wanted. She was

glorious perfection. Slick and hot and ardent. Her tongue glided tauntingly over him, her lips milking him, dragging him closer and closer to ecstasy, until he cried out in blessed release and spent fully down her throat. "Hell and damnation," he gasped.

She clambered up him, kissing him hard, giving him a good taste of himself on her lips. When she pulled away, she wore an impish grin that made his heart wobble.

"You moan exceedingly well," she said. "I don't know if I can match that."

Jack knew a challenge when he heard one. He grasped her waist and rolled them both over, setting her on a step and hiking up her nightgown. "I will do my absolute best to assist you with that, my ravenous temptress."

She needed no further prompting to spread her legs, giving him access to her core, moist and ready for his questing fingers. He began slowly, exploring her with gentle caresses, until she wriggled against him in a silent plea for more.

"Yes, beautiful," he whispered. "I have much more for you."

He replaced his fingers with his mouth, and her response was instantaneous and afire with passion. Her hips bucked and her hands clutched at the stone steps, as if to prevent herself from flying away. "Jack. Oh, heavens," she gasped.

He lavished attention on her clit, lashing it with tiny licks and sucking it until she writhed, low, delicious moans bursting from her throat.

"Yes, oh yes."

He eased first one finger, then a second inside her, thrusting as he sucked, matching his timing to the rhythm she set as she rocked into him. She clenched around his fingers, soaking them with the wet rush of her climax, her entire body tightening and then unfurling in a long, glorious convulsion of bliss.

Jack wiped his mouth on the hem of her nightgown and crawled up beside her, still not caring that the steps beneath them were cold and hard, or that his shoulder had cramped up a bit from the unusual position. Tess was in his arms, and he'd tasted heaven. Nothing else mattered.

He kissed her and pressed his cheek to hers. "Now will you let me into your room for the night?"

She sighed. "I think we'd best separate before we are discovered. But perhaps tomorrow we can arrange a visit. We may have to repeat the moaning contest. I'm unsure which of us won."

Jack laughed and kissed her again. "I believe we both did."

17

Cups

TESS WOKE TO A KNOCK on her door and bolted upright. Jack? He would be wildly foolish to come calling first thing in the morning when the entire household was rising, but at the same time her heart fluttered madly with the hope of seeing him. The door swung open, and a young chambermaid slipped inside. Tess exhaled slowly, half in relief, half disappointment.

"Beg pardon, miss," the girl said, executing an awkward curtsey, "but we've been sent to tell all the guests breakfast will be formal today. I'll see to your hearth and then be on my way unless you need assistance with dressing?"

"No, I can manage on my own, thank you."

The girl poked about a bit in the fireplace, leaving a low-burning fire that Tess didn't think necessary. She curtsied again and hurried off.

Tess rose and dressed in one of the same simple dresses she always wore, looking herself over in the mirror. Her clothes were modest and not fancy, but they were cut to emphasize her figure rather than hide it. She'd never entirely suppressed her rebellious streak. Funny how no one had seemed to notice until Jack Weaver came along.

This unexpected formal breakfast roused her suspicion, so she tucked a folded piece of paper and a miniature pencil into the watch pocket in her bodice, just in case she needed to jot a few notes.

Tess had risen late—as she usually did these days, thanks to her late-night adventures—and was one of the last to enter the dining room. A place awaited her between Sir Cyril Montague and Rowland the Not-So-Magnificent. It was also uncomfortably far from Jack, Lydia, and Ginny. Tess gave her neighbors a half-hearted smile and took her seat.

Despite the formal setting, the food was the same fare she'd seen every morning laid out on the sideboard in the breakfast room. Tess picked at it while pretending not to understand Rowland's none-too-subtle innuendos about sausages. This was not the morning she'd envisioned following the most exciting night of her life. She'd been wise not to let Jack come to her room. If he'd been there when the maid had entered, Tess could have found herself ruined once again.

"Good morning, everyone." The tone of Bardrick's announcement suggested he thought this morning the complete antithesis of good. "Since you are all gathered here, I would like to inform you of some small alterations to our party in preparation for the upcoming finale and announcement of who, if anyone, has won the prize. I'm sure you are aware that this event will be a night-long gala with more than one hundred additional guests joining us for the celebration. As such, safety and security of all guests and of the castle itself are of highest priority. It has been brought to my attention that unknown persons have been moving about the castle at night."

Sir Cyril shifted nervously in the seat beside Tess. Poor man. She didn't fault him and his wife for playing sex games in the kitchens. Especially not when she and Jack had been sucking each other off on the tower stairs last night.

"It seems there was an attempted burglary," Bardrick continued. "Therefore, certain of my footmen have been assigned overnight watch to prevent any criminal mischief, and if any of you are seen leaving your chambers after the party has retired for the night, you will be asked to return at once if you do not wish to be charged with a crime. It is unfortunate that circumstances have led to this, but I cannot allow such underhandedness to occur on my property."

His gaze drifted back and forth across the table, lingering on each of the spiritualists. Damn him and his arrogant hypocrisy. He would condemn others as liars and cheats, when he himself was running a far bigger scam?

Tess crushed her napkin between her fingers below the table, looking anywhere but at Jack. She longed to know what he was thinking at that very moment. Any hopes for another nighttime encounter had been dashed. Did he feel the disappointment as keenly as she did?

"You. Photographer," Bardrick snapped.

Tess's control shattered. Her gaze darted to Jack, who sat at the opposite end of the table, his posture one of casual indifference, a teacup held lazily in his hand. He didn't so much as glance at her.

"You are to finish your photos of the castle," Bardrick ordered. "Then gather all the prints of both the castle and myself and arrange them in an appropriate order to be gathered into a book. Haverstock will be writing explanations to accompany each image."

Lord Haverstock jumped. "I will?" He straightened up. "I mean, yes. As your dear friend I would be more than happy to contribute. And with spirit photographs as fine and intricate…"

"And majestic!" Sir Cyril interrupted, near enough to Tess's ear that she winced. "So masterfully done. Grand enough to be paraded before the whole kingdom."

"Perhaps we might consider compensating Mr. Weaver for his time and effort producing the images for us all," Tess said softly. "He is, after all, a skilled craftsman, and should receive payment for his work."

Good Lord, I've lost my mind.

How had she gone from determination to expose his tricks to the world to insisting he be paid for his fabricated photos? She wasn't even certain anymore who was a victim. No one? Everyone? Her black and white world had fused into a murky gray.

The thought of writing her articles caused a painful knot in her gut. She didn't know what she would say, or even if she could write anything at all. On the other hand, with the guests under scrutiny and no more opportunity for friskiness with Jack, she would have plenty of time.

How depressing.

By the next afternoon, Tess had written and rewritten her article so many times that words and phrases caromed around in her brain like billiard balls. Her attempts to arrange them in some semblance of order lasted no more than a few minutes, and then they were off again, scattered here and there, as disordered as her muddled mind. Her eyes ached. Her head throbbed. The queasy feeling in her gut wouldn't go away.

Even a change of setting hadn't helped. The elegant writing desk in the sun-drenched sitting room had done nothing to ease her struggles.

"You look as though you need a break, Miss Cochran," Ginny said gently, causing Tess's head to snap up. "I'm sure your correspondents wouldn't wish you to wear yourself out simply so a letter might arrive a single day sooner."

"Yes, you are right, of course." Tess folded the papers and tucked them away into the small bag where she stored her writing supplies. "Perhaps a walk." She slung the bag over her shoulder. Maybe she could return to the beach and prepare a plan for catching the orchid smugglers in action.

"Excellent. The whole party is going out to the gardens. You can join us."

Tess almost spun around and walked the other way, but Ginny caught her arm.

"You must join us, Tess," she whispered. "People are talking."

"What?"

"Come along," Ginny said cheerfully, threading her arm

through Tess's and leaning in as if they were lifelong friends swapping secrets. "I have so much to tell you."

"What do you mean, 'people are talking'?" Tess demanded, the moment they were alone among the flowers, safely out of earshot of the other guests.

"About you and Mr. Weaver, of course. You two haven't spoken for days, and word is you broke his heart."

"Nonsense. We have spoken, and quite cordially." *And much, much more.* "Simply in private."

Ginny smiled her meddlesome smile. "I thought so. He doesn't seem upset to me. More... determined. But the rumors say you are writing love letters to some other man and that is why you will not talk to him. In public."

"I'm not writing love letters."

Ginny laughed. "Oh, I know that! I know exactly what you're writing. Well, not *exactly*, but I know who you are and why you're here. And I believe I even know why you're having trouble."

Tess stiffened. "Just who are you, Lady Virginia?"

"I'm a woman who wants to see other women succeed in life. And I'm a friend. Never doubt that. Oh, but I'm afraid I must now confess to a certain underhandedness. I lured you out here not only so that I might give you a much-needed respite from your work, but to put you directly in Mr. Weaver's path. I believe he's been hoping to see you alone. Talk to him. It might help."

Ginny released her and scampered away.

Tess remained frozen in place, watching Jack striding toward her, a rainbow-colored bouquet clutched in his hands. They were some distance removed from most of the party, but hardly alone. Anyone could see them. Tess didn't look to see if all eyes were on her, but it certainly felt as if they were.

"Miss Cochran," Jack's formal address and the bow he gave her were so wildly different from the way he'd moaned her name during their lovemaking that for an instant Tess thought perhaps she had dreamed the entire encounter. Or was this the dream? She might have fallen asleep over her hopeless writing.

Jack held out the flowers. "I picked these for you."

Tess accepted the bouquet, but her lips puckered in confusion. "What are you doing?"

"Courting you."

Her eyes went wide. "What?"

"Bardrick has made it difficult to arrange midnight meetings, but I value our time together. Therefore, I have come a-courting."

"Are you mad?"

His mouth twisted in a wry grin. "I suspect so, yes."

"Jack, this is ridiculous. No one is going to believe…"

"That I might have more than a passing interest in you?" His blue eyes darkened with passion, boring into her. His tongue snaked over his lips, setting a blaze of desire rushing through her. "They already do, beautiful. I won't let Bardrick ruin our friendship or thwart our ability to speak to one another privately. But you may thwart me, if you so desire. Will you receive my attentions? Or shall I give up hope?"

"Jack…" Tess lifted the flowers to her nose and inhaled deeply, letting the fragrant perfume soothe her troubled mind. "Why are you truly here? We have nothing we need to discuss. I have no regrets about the other night, and while I'm sorry it can't happen again, we both know we'll soon go our separate ways. We have simply been separated sooner than anticipated."

His expression didn't change, his lips still curving in the casual half-smirk he wore so easily, but the spark in his eyes died, leaving them cold as ice. Her words had upset him. Not long ago, such a change would have passed right by her, unheeded. Now, though, she recognized the subtle signs of his inner thoughts.

"I know," she sighed. "I'm disappointed too. I truly had planned to invite you to my bedroom."

He only shook his head and looked away, not saying anything, his hands clasped behind his back.

"Maybe we can slip away together during the party." Wishful thinking. People would be everywhere. They stood a better chance of dashing across the hall when the bored footmen weren't watching.

"The party is a cover-up," Jack said, still not looking at her.

"For a big orchid shipment? I agree. I can think of no other reason for Bardrick to host such an event. I don't think he's become a believer. I suspect he spread the original tales of hauntings to account for the noises in the night caused by the orchid creation and earlier transactions. Now he plans to use the chaos of the party and the 'proof' of spirits to disguise any noises or odd comings and goings."

"Exactly. Gather a large group of spiritual believers, get them thoroughly liquored up, and they'll swear on their grandmothers' graves it's all ghosts."

"And by giving up such a huge sum as five thousand pounds, he gives serious social credence to the notion that his house is truly haunted."

Jack turned to face her at last. "Leaving him with the ability to continue his fake orchid smuggling indefinitely. The only question remaining is: do you intend to do anything about it?"

"Yes." Tess hadn't decided until that very moment, but she was certain now. She needed to follow up on the smuggling story. Her spiritualist reveal was going nowhere. But if she could prove Bardrick's involvement and discover who his buyer was, she could throw the other story away entirely. No one would care about fake spirit photos when they could read about an earl swindling his own kind. "I want to catch them in the act."

"I think we can do that. But it will take preparation."

"Yes. We have some time to plan, fortunately."

"We will need to talk, you and I," Jack said. "Privately."

Their eyes met. A bit of the ice faded from his gaze. "May I court you? It will give us the opportunity to talk."

A convenient courtship that couldn't lead anywhere. He'd be gone in a matter of days, and she'd be heading back to her ordinary life, hopefully with a good story.

"Yes, you may."

"Thank you." He bowed to her again. "Have a pleasant afternoon, Miss Cochran. I hope you enjoy the flowers. And I hope you will assist me during the party for Lord Bardrick's final photo."

"I would like that."

She watched him leave, once again feeling the loss of his presence as a pang in her belly. In a few days she would watch him walk away forever. Tess lifted her bouquet again, brushing the soft petals against her cheek, and letting the delicate fragrance soak into her. Hearts were mad, foolish things. And right now hers wanted nothing more than for the courtship to be real.

18
Wheel of Fortune

JACK EXECUTED A SWEEPING BOW better suited for the court of mid-eighteenth century France. Perhaps he ought to have gone into the theater.

"May I have this dance, milady?"

Tess stared at him with that analytical gaze of hers. The one that said not, "You're peculiar," but, "*Why* are you peculiar?" Jack loved that look. It meant he challenged her and she wanted to understand him. If he could earn a lifetime of that look, he'd be the happiest of men.

"I don't believe any of us are meant to dance," she replied.

Jack glanced at the pianoforte. "Then why has Lady Virginia struck up a waltz?" He extended a hand. "Shall we?"

Tess placed her hand in his without hesitation and his heart soared. Two days of ardent courtship had left their mark. Hopefully Bardrick wouldn't notice the other mark they'd left on the gardens. Jack might have picked a few more flowers than was prudent.

"I actually don't know how to dance," he admitted, drawing her into his arms and setting them both into motion. "All I know is the waltz goes one-two-three and spins a bit."

Tess laughed. "You are doing a reasonable approximation, except you began with the wrong foot. I'm all turned around." She stepped on him, they stumbled, and had to restart, this time beginning with the correct foot.

"I'm improvising based entirely on what I've seen others do. Fortunately, I do have a good sense of rhythm."

"You could be a fine dancer if you learned and practiced."

"I would practice day and night if you would be my partner." The words came easily and unrehearsed. He no longer thought about what he said to Tess, the way he did with others. He simply spoke. He hoped she wasn't tired of hearing such compliments, because he couldn't have stopped if he tried.

Their bodies settled into the movements, and he dared to bring her closer. Her eyes were warm liquid pools, shining with pleasure. Soft, pink lips parted just enough to beg for a kiss. He'd managed to sneak a few over the past two days, but nothing more. His body ached for her.

"This is outrageous," she said. Her smiling face made Jack vow to do at least one outrageous thing every day.

"And you love it." *Can you love me?* "Are you prepared for tonight?"

Her smile thinned a bit and her eyes hardened. "Yes. This dress has pockets. I have everything I need with me. Are you certain you can keep Phantom quiet?"

"Yes. I took some extra chicken at lunch so I would have a snack for her."

"Good. After this dance is over, we will be calm and respectable for the remainder of the evening. And we will not retire at the same time."

"I will meet you there, then. Watch for guards and be careful."

"You don't need to patronize me."

The music was winding down, so Jack came to a halt and lifted her hand to his lips. "I'm not. I'm merely worrying about you because I care." He pressed a kiss to her knuckles. "This is risky."

"I know. But it's something I need to do." Tess withdrew her hand from his grasp and backed away. "Thank you for the lovely dance."

Why? he wondered as she walked off. *Why do you need to do this?*

The orchid smuggling was fascinating, certainly, but it had no bearing on her assignment. She was to write about the spiritualists. Expose them. Expose *him*. Jack was certain she knew at least a couple of his methods for producing spirit photographs, though she had never caught him at any of them. Was that the trouble? Did she worry her story wasn't good enough and she needed something more?

His stomach flip-flopped. Damn. He didn't want to be the reason she lost her job. He would help her with her quest for this smuggling story, however risky it might be. She could use it to replace the spiritualist exposé, and they both would walk away from the party with jobs and reputations intact. And once he had those five thousand pounds, he'd confess his feelings for her.

He spent the remainder of the evening at cards, winning a modest amount without any cheating, while casting flirtatious glances across the room at Tess. Her smile was a thing of beauty. She'd smiled often during his admittedly over-the-top courtship. They'd planned her mad upcoming adventure, but they'd also talked. Blue was her favorite color. She loved most fruits but not strawberries. She enjoyed reading tales of far-away lands and had once seen a real tiger at a traveling circus show. Her laugh made him melt a little inside.

Jack retired from the evening activities first, using the excuse of quitting before his luck ran out. He stopped to bid Tess goodnight, kissing her hand again despite all the eyes on him—many of them disapproving.

With the household still active, he couldn't walk directly to the conservatory, but a round-about path that began heading toward his bedchamber eventually brought him to the appropriate hall unnoticed. Jack peeked around the corner. A sleepy footman leaned against the wall, guarding the conservatory door.

Jack backed away to the nearest room and slipped inside. A few minutes later, Tess joined him.

"One guard," he whispered. "Are you absolutely certain you want to do this? If we're caught we could be charged with trespassing or worse."

"I'm certain. But why are *you* doing this?"

"Because every adventuress needs an accomplice. Ready?"

She raised an eyebrow in skepticism, but then nodded. Jack opened the door. He counted to three, then thumped the door with a fist, hard enough to rattle it. Tess screamed.

"Help!" she shrieked.

"Shut up, bitch," Jack snarled.

Tess jogged in place, her feet pounding the ground to create audible footsteps. "No! Stop! Help!"

Jack faked running after her, letting his stomps fade away before taking Tess by the arm and ducking back inside the room.

The sound of boots slapping on the floor rushed past. "Who's there? Where are you? Show yourself!"

Praying the ruse would hold, Jack hurried from the room, Tess pressed close to his side. A glance around the corner flooded him with relief. The guard was gone. Step one accomplished. They opened the conservatory door, hurried inside, and made their way through the foliage to the center of the room.

Now, they waited.

～〇

The floor was cold and Tess's leg was cramping up, but the fact that the entire length of Jack's body was pressed against hers made up for it. Two days of fleeting touches had been agony. Their waltz had been heavenly, though it had left her burning with desire.

Now she was selfishly hoping Bardrick didn't show. She could happily lie here snuggling with Jack and watching him pet a kitten until she fell asleep. Later, she would wake in his arms and he would make love to her until dawn.

The conservatory door opened. Son of a bitch.

From her hiding place on the floor, Tess could see little glimpses of Bardrick as he moved between the worktables, checking over the orchids and making small changes to some of the plants. Tess jotted down everything she saw while Jack kept Phantom calm and quiet with cuddles and snacks.

Time passed. Tess's leg ached, and she had an itch on one elbow she didn't dare scratch. Bardrick repeated the same procedure with orchid after orchid, so she had nothing more to write. Her eyelids drooped. She blinked hard, trying to fight the sleepiness.

The sound of the door lock turning startled her, and Bardrick, too, from the sudden curse he blurted.

"Who's there? Show yourself!"

"For God's sake, man, you'll rouse the household shouting like that," a familiar voice replied.

Rowland? What in hell was he doing here? Tess glanced at Jack, who twitched one shoulder in the tiniest of shrugs. She readied her notebook.

"What are you doing here?" Bardrick snarled. "And what right do you have to address me in so insolent a fashion? Was it you who's been sneaking about?"

"I've done nothing. We had a bargain. I want my payment."

"You've received your payment, magician. You'll need better tricks if you want more."

Tess could see half of Rowland's face between plants. His mouth twisted into a furious snarl. "I've heard rumors," he spat.

"This house is full of rumors."

"Rumors about the money. Rumors you intend to give the five thousand to the brat with the camera."

"He has talent. The eye of an artist and a knack for capturing spirits."

"It's nothing but trickery," Rowland insisted. Far better trickery than he'd ever accomplished, that was certain.

"We shall see. Tomorrow I shall summon a spirit of my

own choosing. If he captures it correctly, he will have earned the prize."

Rowland stalked toward Bardrick so forcefully that Bardrick put out a hand and shoved him away.

"That money is mine!" Rowland snarled.

"No. I hired you to suggest ways to make my house appear haunted and to spread talk of it in town. You were compensated for your work. This contest and this affair are mine and mine alone. Your failure to impress me with your performances is of your own making. I promised you nothing. Now get out."

"You can't do this to me!"

"Get out before I turn you over to the authorities. I'm certain they can find you a cozy little cell in Newgate Prison."

Jack shuddered, and Tess's gaze darted to him. Had he gone pale? The darkness made it difficult to tell. She rubbed her arm against his in what she hoped was a reassuring manner.

Rowland turned and stomped away. "Go to the devil, Bardrick," he called.

"You may inform him that I'm coming. But after a much longer and wealthier life than yours."

Rowland didn't say another word. A few moments later, the conservatory door slammed.

"Fool," Bardrick muttered. "I should never have invited him." He turned back to the table. "One more night and he'll be gone. And so will all of you, my beauties." He waved a hand over the array of orchids. "Pay five thousand to earn three times as much. And the promise of continuing payouts for years to come. Perhaps that Madame Xyla could be a winner also. She did make an excellent prediction."

Ten minutes later, Bardrick declared his work finished and departed. Tess and Jack remained motionless, waiting in the darkness and silence until they felt sure the earl had left for good.

"Jesus," Jack swore.

"So Rowland was part of it," Tess mused. "And Bardrick's

words confirm everything we suspected: the hauntings and the prize are to conceal the smuggling operation. This is excellent."

"I think he might want to kill me."

"What?" Tess looked at Jack for a long moment. He was still a bit paler than usual.

"Did you see Rowland's face? He looked ready to murder someone. Fuck." Jack ran a hand through his hair. "If Bardrick awards me that money… I never thought this would be dangerous."

Phantom mewled, perhaps sensing his agitation.

"He can't hurt you in front of all the guests," Tess assured him. "Keep your door locked tonight."

"You know how worthless those locks are."

She did. She'd broken into his room in a matter of seconds, and she'd never picked a lock before in her life. Tess reached out and covered Jack's hand with her own, squeezing gently.

"Then stay with me tonight."

"Are you certain? It's one more risk on top of all the others. Your luck won't hold forever."

She looked him straight in the eye. Whatever happened, she would not let him come to harm. "Your life is worth the risk."

19

Death

TESS CHOKED BACK A CRY as Jack yanked his coat up over his head and tore off down the hall, bellowing like a drunkard.

Damn you, Jack Weaver, why are you so foolishly gallant?

He hadn't asked her about this plan ahead of time, knowing she would have forbidden it. But now that he was running around like a lunatic, taking the hall guards with him, she would have to be more foolish than he was not to take advantage. She slipped quietly into her room and leaned against the wall beside the door, waiting.

She dug her fingers into the cloth of her skirts, twisting and crushing the fabric. She would never be able to relax until either her door or his opened. This evening's mischief had been all her idea, but he had tagged along without question, for no good reason she could see. Did danger and drama simply appeal to him? She wondered if he saw all the world as a great stage show where he alternately played the dashing hero and the comic relief.

Interminable minutes later, the door handle turned and Jack ducked into her room. "All clear," he announced. "I led the guards on a merry chase, but I don't think they had any idea who I was. We should be safe until morning."

Tess locked the door, little good it would do. "Please don't do anything like that again. I nearly shouted when you ran off, and I don't like to think of what might have happened if you'd been caught."

"I wasn't worried about being caught. Besides, I won't need to do it again."

"Of course. Tonight is the last night before..." She choked on the words. *The last night before the party. The last night before the end. The last night before we part forever.*

The light in the room was too dim to read his expression, but he was still and silent for what seemed like hours.

"Well," he said at last, "I suppose we shouldn't waste any time, then, should we?" He shrugged out of his coat and tossed it onto a chair.

Tess yanked on the buttons of her bodice, swept up in an urgent, desperate need to be rid of all barriers between them. The clothing they both ordinarily took such care with began to fly, thrown off or dropped to the floor as they shed layer after layer. By the time Tess reached her bedside, she was down to her chemise and stockings. She turned up the bedside lamp to its brightest, wanting to see all of him when at last they came together.

She hiked up her shift, reaching to untie her garter and giving him a coy smile... and froze. Jack was fully naked, and in the glow of the lamplight she could see every bit of his pale skin, including the long, red slash running across his abdomen.

"What happened to you?" she blurted, too stunned to consider the rudeness of the question before she spoke.

"Nothing. It's nothing."

He moved toward her, but she stopped him with an outstretched hand. "Virtual disembowelment is not nothing. Who hurt you?" Whoever it was, she wanted to hurt them back. The force of her fury stunned her. She sat heavily on the bed. "I hate whoever it was. Is that wrong of me? Is that crazy?"

Jack sat beside her. "I don't even know his name. He's probably dead, anyway."

"How did it happen?"

He took her hand in his, rubbing his thumb in small circles across the back of her hand. Their eyes met. His were hard and serious, but with something more beneath. A shimmer of pain, perhaps?

She shouldn't press him. Forcing him to relive what must have been a traumatic incident was cruel. Tess was opening her mouth to tell him he needn't say another word when he spoke.

"I'll give you my secrets for yours."

Her response rushed from her lungs in a breathless gasp. "Yes. Please."

"I grew up in a gambling house," Jack began. "My father and uncle owned it together. They both became enamored of an actress who performed at a nearby theater, and they went one night to visit her, thinking to discover which of them she might prefer. Instead they discovered twins, each of whom was immediately taken with one of the brothers. Courtship ensued, then marriages, then little cousins, born only three months apart.

"Lydia and I lived among cards and dice, learning how to stack a deck and how to read an opponent alongside the usual letters and arithmetic. We were heirs to a gambling legacy, and if it was an unusual life for a pair of children, we didn't know. It was normal to us and we were happy."

Tess leaned against him, pressing her shoulder into his. She could picture little Lydia and Jack, running around and laughing. Mischievous, clever, adorable.

Jack's expression tightened. "When I was eight, an argument broke out at the club. That wasn't rare, but this incident involved weapons. My father made the mistake of trying to halt the violence. He was murdered for his troubles. The sudden shock of it affected my mother so badly that she fell ill and never recovered. A year later she was gone."

He stared off into space as he talked, his voice calm, but with an undercurrent of abiding sadness. Tess gave his hand a reassuring squeeze.

You are not alone.

"Lydia's parents took me in, of course, but the year we were thirteen a devastating fire broke out at the club. My aunt and uncle weren't able to escape. It burned to the ground, leaving us with nothing. All on our own, we had to rely on the skills we had: gambling. In particular, cheating to ensure we would win. I was good, but Lydia was an expert. Unfortunately, we soon discovered that unlike our club, most gambling halls didn't admit women, and only the sleaziest of places let in anyone as young as we were. I had to do most of the work, and one day, shortly after my seventeenth birthday, I got caught." He let out a long, slow breath. "I don't like to talk about this."

Tess released his hand, wrapping an arm around him instead. "You don't have to," she assured him. "You can stop at any time. I won't pressure you."

He squeezed his eyes briefly closed. "No, I have to tell someone, and I'd like it to be you. For two and a half years, I was incarcerated at Newgate Prison. I can't even begin to explain how awful it was. I'm sure you've heard stories. This..." He ran a finger across his scar. "Happened early on. I tried to intervene to break up a fight. I may look like my mother, but I'm very much my father's son. Fortunately, the knife only skimmed me, or I would have been eviscerated. They left me for dead. Dumped me in a tiny, dark cell. Stone walls with water seeping in and rats scuttling, and I just lay there, knowing I would die. Somehow I didn't."

He began to shiver, so Tess pulled the coverlet off the bed and wrapped it around him. She couldn't tell if he was cold or simply haunted by the memories, but she would do whatever she could to comfort him.

"I was ill for a long time," he continued. "Don't know that I ever fully recovered. As you can see, I'm not particularly a tower of strength." He gestured at his lanky body.

Tess embraced him, pressing a kiss to his cheek. "I think you're beautiful, and anyone who can live through hell and come out as well as you have done has strength far beyond the mere physical."

He lifted one shoulder in that half-shrug of his. "I still have nightmares at times. And that smuggler's tunnel makes me tremble. Dark, cramped places bring back the memories."

Tess held him as he fell silent, not wanting to rush him or pressure him. When the silence began to stretch out, she asked softly, "Is there more, or shall I tell you a story now?"

"You know the rest. I run cons because I'm good at reading people. I sold my body for extra money. I bought a camera and learned to use it because that's what I really love."

Tess straightened up and shifted her position on the bed to better look him in the eye. "I'm not an orphan," she confessed. "At least I don't think so. When I was young, my father would come and go. I didn't understand why, but I thought it was his job and my mother and I were happy, especially the times he was with us. But then my mother died of a sudden illness, and I was sent to a school for orphaned girls."

Jack regarded her with a solemn frown. "Your father never came for you."

She shook her head. "I kept saying to the others that there must have been some mistake. I had a father and he would take me home. But he didn't. I began to hear the whispers. Words like 'bastard' and 'mistress' that I had never heard before. It wasn't long before I came to understand them. In desperation I asked the teachers about my father, begging for any news, any hope that such things might not be true and he might be coming for me. Eventually I was taken aside and told that my father had a 'real' family who required his attention and I was to consider myself orphaned as much as any of the girls. They wouldn't even tell me his name."

Jack muttered a curse under his breath and her heart swelled with affection for him.

"Ever since, I've wondered if someday I might stumble into my father and recognize him. I rehearsed what I might say. I would rail at him for his deceit and his abandonment. I would pour out all my anger until he felt the guilt and shame for his misdeeds as deeply as I feel his betrayal."

Jack hauled her into his lap, adjusting the blanket to wrap it around them both. "My poor, sweet Tess. Is this why lies are so abhorrent to you? Why you seek the truth in everything?"

"Yes."

"Know this for the truth, then: only a fool would desert you. He never deserved you, the scoundrel. I would pummel him, if I knew his name."

Tess blinked away a stray tear. "I want to pummel the man who knifed you. We're quite the bloodthirsty pair, it seems."

He gave her a sad smile and brushed his lips to her cheek. "I wish so dearly I could take away your pain."

"I feel the same."

His mouth moved onto hers, kissing gently, reverently. "What I can do is bring you pleasure, if you desire."

Tess gripped him tightly. "Yes. Please."

Nothing could have prepared Tess for this. Gone was the frenzied hunger that had swept them away on the tower stairs. The wild, frantic heat possessing her before they had spilled their secrets had transformed into something new and strange. A deep, simmering need to be close to him, not for a moment, but for all time.

If only.

Jack's hands traversed her skin in slow, worshipful strokes, as if this one night could linger into forever. Tess wished it would.

"What in all nine circles of hell did I ever do to deserve this?" Jack murmured. He pressed a kiss to her neck, inching downward with hands and lips.

"You're a darling man," she replied.

His laughter against her skin made her body sing with delight. "The good sort of scoundrel?"

"The best." Tess threaded her fingers through his hair as his tongue lazily laved her nipple. Her eyes slipped closed. "Though I do like it when you're wicked, too."

"For you, love, I will be as wicked as you desire."

Love. The word thrummed inside her, growing stronger with each kiss and caress. He was loving her with skilled lips and fingers, exciting not only her body, but her heart. And she was falling. Tumbling, crashing, her world upended.

If she were to remain Tess the Truth-seeker, she couldn't lie to herself. She was in love with the most inappropriate of men. A man she shouldn't trust, though she longed to from the furthest depths of her heart.

"Jack," she gasped, his name part prayer, part plea.

"Mmm," was all the reply he could make.

Her hands trailed over his back and his shoulders, grasping him, tugging him upward until she brought their mouths together and he settled himself between her legs.

"I don't have any sheaths," he warned her.

Tess rocked her hips against him, the urgency building inside her as his heavy erection rubbed over her slick sex. "I don't care."

He would be careful. She knew this as assuredly as she knew the sun would rise in the morning. And in the event of a blond-haired, blue-eyed accident, he would be devoted and responsible. Nothing like her father. Never.

"I want you, Jack." She kissed him hard, her tongue mimicking the motions she wanted from their bodies. Her hands clamped down over his buttocks, driving his hips into hers, begging him.

Jack wrenched his lips from hers. His hand cupped her cheek and he gazed into her eyes with such intensity that her foolish heart threatened to beat out of her chest. He pushed into her, his eyes never leaving hers, his lips parting on a sigh as their bodies joined.

"Fuck, Tess. Oh, Christ, you feel good."

"Yes. More."

Tess clung to him as he began to move within her, their bodies dancing together, setting a rhythm as easily as if they'd been lovers for years. The tension climbed inside her, higher than she'd thought possible. She flung blankets aside, her body boiling, combusting from the mad heat of their union. Sweat glistened on Jack's brow. And through it all, he stared into her eyes. Stared as if she were his world and he'd forgotten what lay beyond this shared bed.

Tess whimpered, unable to form a more coherent sound. She was drowning in his gaze, burning from his heat, hotter and hotter and hotter until at long last the explosion took her and she gasped and trembled beneath him.

The loss of his presence inside her devastated her, but then his moan of ecstasy reached her ears and she felt his wet, sticky seed on her belly and the weight of his body atop her, and all was right again. He rolled off her, gathering her close, pressing kisses to her brow and into her hair, murmuring things she couldn't quite hear.

"Jack," she sighed.

"Let me clean you up, love, and then we'll sleep."

"Together." She would not allow him to leave. She would not let this night end. She would hold him as long as possible.

Tears welled in her eyes and she blinked them away. Too soon it would all be over. They would part, as she'd always known they would. But when he left, he would be taking some piece of her with him. Tonight, she would cling to everything she had.

"Together," he promised.

20

Wands

Jack floated through the throng of people, a drink in his hand and a spring in his step. Last night with Tess had been the most spectacular of his life. All day he'd pondered and plotted, considering how to hold onto her when this night was over. Tomorrow morning, when the sun rose, he would be taking Bardrick's final photograph. And then he'd offer Tess the adventure of a lifetime. He'd sail her around the world. Take her anywhere and everywhere. Photograph her with the pyramids. Make love to her in the finest French hotel. Hop a train to the American West and gamble in a saloon while watching a bawdy stage show. No cheating, though. Cowboys carried guns.

Jack gave a flirtatious smile to a pretty woman dripping with real jewels. She fluttered her fan and smiled back.

"I know this is terribly forward, since we haven't been introduced," he said, "but your hair shimmers so perfectly in the candlelight. It ought to be immortalized. Have you ever sat for a photograph?"

Her artificially rosy cheeks grew pinker. "No, I have not, and it is shocking for you to speak to me so boldly." She swatted her fan in his direction. "Did you mean what you said? About my hair?"

"Absolutely." These things always worked best when he had no need to lie. Pick a customer's best feature and compliment it. "I'm a photographer and it's my job to spot beauty everywhere." He produced a card and held it out to her. "I can offer a half-hour session with a single print, or an hour session with three prints. Competitive prices and the highest quality product. I also offer specialty photographs."

She looked the card over. "Spirit photography! Ooh, how exciting! Are you the man who has taken the photos here at the castle?"

"I am indeed."

"Wonderful! I will be in touch. Such a pleasure to have met you, Mr..." She glanced at the card. "Weaver. Enjoy the party!" She tucked the card into her cleavage and gave him a suggestive look before scurrying away.

Jack took another swallow of Bardrick's excellent brandy. Another wealthy customer. This party could spread his name to the highest of circles. Perhaps after he and Tess took their world tour he could become Jack Weaver, photographer to the Queen.

Or maybe he was letting his imagination run wild again.

He continued to wend his way through the crowd, smiling and flirting and handing out cards. The night was off to a brilliant start. By the time the spiritualists began their crowning performances, he would be in good favor with the entire party. Only a single problem nagged at him: where was Tess?

Jack swallowed the last of his drink and handed the empty glass to a passing footman who looked barely out of the schoolroom. Was collecting dirty dishes a step up or down from sitting in a hallway watching for guests who might dare leave their rooms? Both sounded awful, honestly, but the boy did have plenty to eat and a sturdy roof over his head. Jack thanked him.

The footman's eyes widened at the unexpected acknowledgement and he stammered a surprised, "You're very welcome, sir."

"Have you seen Miss Cochran, by any chance?"

"Who?"

Jack sighed. "Never mind." He headed into the next room, determined to find her. She'd told him, before he snuck out of her room at dawn, that she would be wearing her one and only evening gown tonight. All day he'd been fantasizing about it. He hoped the neckline was scandalously low to show off her exquisite bosom.

Dammit, where was she? He'd been wandering the house for an hour and hadn't caught so much as a glimpse of her. She couldn't be out stalking smugglers. The party had only begun and full darkness hadn't even settled yet. He paused and scanned the room, looking for a flash of auburn hair among the minglers.

Jack spied Rowland the Manipulative and wormed his way to the magician's side. "Have you seen Miss Cochran about?"

Rowland's tweezed eyebrows knitted. "Who?"

For God's sake! "The young woman I've been wooing?"

"Oh, her. Can't say I have." He stalked off, a scowl on his face. Jack made a rude gesture to his departing back.

"The library," Jack muttered. "I'll try the library." Tess probably wanted time alone with a book. She didn't enjoy mingling the way he did. Maybe he could sneak a kiss in private.

Jack almost groaned aloud when he stepped into the library to find a dozen guests standing inside chatting. He started to turn back when a flash of emerald green caught his eye. His breath hitched.

There she was. The color of the dress brought out the red in her hair and the low back displayed creamy skin and the elegant column of her neck. He started toward her, heedless of anything in his path, drawn to her like a magnet to iron. He was the lover in a fairytale, striding across a crowded room to sweep his intended into his arms and declare…

"There you are, my dear! How lovely to see you again after all these years!"

Jack jerked to a halt. The older woman who had spoken

stood at Tess's side, a cheery smile on her face. Someone here knew her?

"And you, Lady Goosebury." Tess's voice was warm, happy.

"I was so pleased to have been able to secure an invitation for you, Miss Cochran," Lady Goosebury continued. "When I received your note, I said to myself, 'Ah, Miss Cochran! Such an intelligent and self-reliant young woman.' Indeed, I wondered how you could still be Miss Cochran. You are old enough to have married, and married well if you set your mind to it."

"Oh, no," Tess replied hurriedly. "I can't imagine I'm likely ever to be married."

Jack flexed his fingers, trying to ease the sudden tension that flared up inside him. If she meant no one would ever desire to marry her, she was dead wrong. Because the longer he knew her, the more he craved forever. If she meant she had no desire to marry... well, he would simply have to find a way to work with that.

"I am gainfully employed and seeing to my own welfare, as you taught us," Tess continued. "I'm a journalist, in fact, and I'm here to write a story centered around tonight's events."

Vague. Surprising, though, that she would divulge even that much.

"Miss Cochran," Jack exclaimed, as if just now spying her.

She whirled around at the sound of his voice. Her emerald dress was cut just as low in the front as in the back. A seamstress somewhere deserved a large tip.

"I hope I'm not interrupting," he lied, then followed with a truth, as all practiced conmen did. "I've been looking for you. Won't you do me the honor of introducing me to your friend?"

"Ja— Mr. Weaver. Hello." She turned back to the other woman. "Lady Goosebury, please allow me to present my friend, Mr. Jack Weaver. Mr. Weaver, this is Lady Goosebury, the patroness of the school where I resided for many years."

"Ah! A pleasure, my lady." Jack made a slight bow.

"Excellent work you do. Might I suggest, however, that you include lessons warning young ladies away from photographers? Terrible, roguish sorts they are. Not at all to be trusted. Isn't that correct, Miss Cochran?"

Lady Goosebury arched one eyebrow in much the way Tess often did. He wondered if Tess had unconsciously learned to mimic her mentor. "I gather *you* are a photographer, Mr. Weaver? I must agree wholeheartedly. Stay far away from him, Miss Cochran. He is clearly trouble. Entirely too flirtatious. Enjoy the party, my dear, and when you arrive home, do write me and update me on the result of all this…" She waved a hand at their surroundings, though the gesture was chiefly directed at Jack. "Excitement."

She strode regally from the library, leaving Tess at the mercy of Jack's roguish ways.

"Lady Goosebury, eh?" He smothered a chuckle.

"Please don't make fun of her name. She's a fine lady, and the reason I had the education that got me where I am today."

"And I will forever be thankful for where you are today." He looked straight down into the valley between her breasts. "And for what you are wearing. I might even pray about it. 'Dear Lord, thank you for blessing this poor sinner with such… overflowing bounty.'"

Tess giggled and ran both hands down the smooth silk of the dress. "Oh, do you like it, then?"

"Like is not a strong enough word. In fact, I think the only way to truly express my admiration is to confess that I ought to have worn looser trousers."

She glanced down. Jack swallowed hard. Damn. He wasn't going to last the night at this rate.

He offered Tess his arm. "Shall we dance?"

Her fingers curled around his bicep. "Is there dancing?"

"I hope so, because I want to hold you. If not, we can do whatever you please. Mingle with high society. Drink ourselves silly. Stand in the corner and silently observe the party while avoiding any interaction."

"You would stand in the corner with me?"

"Absolutely."

Her smile made his heart skip a beat. "In that case, I accept your invitation."

They danced. Badly, but joyously. They waltzed in a corner while other music was playing because every other style of dance was even more incomprehensible to him. Jack flirted and mingled with Tess on his arm, handing out more cards. When he sensed her growing tired, they paused in a quiet corner, bodies close together, saying little.

"I love this," he whispered, after several silent minutes of people watching. "I love sharing my world with you and I love being allowed into yours. Truly, I don't know that I've ever been happier."

She stepped close enough for her beauteously displayed breasts to press against his arm. "Jack..." she began.

"Ladies and gentlemen," a voice intoned. "The first of our illustrious spiritualists is prepared for her demonstration. If everyone would gather in the Great Hall, the night's festivities will begin."

Tess gripped Jack's arm. "That's our cue."

He nodded. One final night's plan. They would sneak out separately, meet half-way to the beach, and watch for the orchid smugglers. Tess would have the last piece of her story.

"Bring a blanket. I'd hate for your gorgeous dress to be damaged. You needn't worry about cold, though. I'll keep you warm."

She leaned into him, only for a moment. "Perhaps afterward we can find time to be alone."

"Please."

They abandoned their corner and followed the mass of people moving toward the Great Hall. A few people weren't joining the main group, and Jack broke off along with them, the first to depart for the secret rendezvous.

His escape was simple. He walked out to the gardens with several others and began wandering the paths, taking in the night air. As one did when hoping for a private, outdoor tryst.

The gardens were peaceful in the dark, and he walked for quite some time, moving slowly toward the rear of the castle while avoiding the area from which suspicious sighs and heaving breaths emanated. Sir Cyril and Lady Montague, perhaps?

Jack was no more than ten paces from rounding the back of the castle when a cry went up from far behind him.

"Fire!"

He whirled around.

"Out! Out! Away from the castle!"

Fire! Sound the alarm! Get the children out! The distant memory flickered in and out of his mind in an instant, leaving behind only the chill of fear and the scent of smoke in his nostrils.

He jolted. No, the scent was real. His heart began to race.

Jack tore through the gardens, flowers crumpling beneath his boots as he ran across beds and leapt over bushes, taking the straightest path possible. Guests streamed from the doors, their frightened shouts an indecipherable swell of noise. Only a few words broke free of the clamor: *Fire. Out. Away.*

"Tess!" Jack screamed. "Tess, where are you? Lydia!" He pushed through the unruly mob until he found a man who had been with the party from the first. "Have you seen Miss Cochran?" he asked.

"Who?"

"Goddammit! Tess! Tess, are you here? Lydia! Where are you?"

"Jack!" His cousin's voice rang out above the din as she hurried toward him. "Jack, thank God," she gasped. "When I heard about the fire, I thought you might be in danger."

"Lydia, where's Tess? Is she in there? I need to find her." He pushed his way toward the entrance, shoving panicked guests aside as he fought his way against the flow.

She grabbed him by the coat. "Jack, stop. You can't go in there. She'll be fine. They're evacuating everyone."

He pushed her off. "No. I have to find her. I have to see her."

"Jack—"

A large hand clamped down on his shoulder, turning him away from the house. "This way, sir. All guests must move a safe distance from the building while the situation is seen to."

Jack squirmed in the man's grasp, trying to break free from his vise-like grip. "Let me go, damn you! I have to find her!"

A second man grabbed his opposite arm. "Not to worry, sir. The fire began in the parlor area. No guests were nearby."

Jack twisted and jerked, but the men were too strong. "Please," he begged. "Please let me find her."

They hauled him through the garden, ignoring his protests. He thrashed and fought, screaming in terror-stricken fury. "You fucking rat bastards, I will kill you!" Heads turned to gape at him in horror, but he didn't let up. "If anything has happened to her, I'll rip off your bollocks and shove them down your throats, you shit-eating sons of whores!"

"For God's sake, let him go," Lydia shouted.

They did, at last, dumping him in a puddle in the road and looming over him, hands on hips, dark silhouettes of condemnation in the moonlight.

"Don't move," one of them ordered.

"I'll find her, Jack," Lydia assured him. "I'll bring her to you. I'm sure she's safe. She's strong and sensible."

He nodded dumbly. Tess probably hadn't even been inside when the fire had broken out. She was probably half-way to the beach, waiting for him, wondering what all the noise was about.

None of that eased the panic in his heart. He crossed his arms over his chest, trembling.

Fire! Sound the alarm! Get the children out! The memories were vague. Those few words. A flickering glow. The acrid smell of smoke. He'd been half-asleep, scared, confused. By the time he and Lydia had been dragged from the apartment by a neighbor, it was too late. The club next door was doomed and their family gone.

A feline screech cut through the haze of fear. "Phantom?" He turned toward the sound. "Here, girl. I'm here." The kitten scampered toward him, and he gathered her in his arms, stroking her soft fur. "That's my girl."

More of his panic subsided as the cat purred and snuggled against him. Words from earlier finally filtered into his brain. "Wait. Did someone say the parlor?"

"That's where the fire began," one of his guards replied. "Something about chemicals."

Oh, God. His darkroom. All the photos. His equipment. His camera.

"No," Jack gasped.

His life crumbled. He had no more chance to win the five thousand pounds. No more livelihood. No hopes and dreams. Nothing.

"Tess," he moaned. "Tess, where are you?"

21
Judgement

"You realize, Miss Cochran, that now you will never be rid of me." Ginny linked her arm with Tess's and leaned close, her conspiratorial grin lighting the room. "You have enlisted me as an accomplice to your secret tryst, and now we must be friends forever."

"I think we will be. And while I cannot divulge any details tonight, I promise soon you will hear the whole story."

Soon the world will hear the story. The arrogant nobleman, exposed to all.

Bardrick might be forced to withdraw from society, but he would survive. The loss of his prestige would be punishment enough. More importantly, Jack and Lydia wouldn't be out on the street. Perhaps Jack would even win the money and be able to retire from a life of swindling.

A girl could dream.

A giddy shiver ran down her spine and Tess fought for composure. No ridiculous daydreams. Life wasn't a fairytale. She had to be rational, and the rational conclusion was that she and Jack weren't meant to be. No matter how much she wished otherwise. He was a swindler. She exposed such people. End of story.

"It's so romantic," Ginny sighed. "You and Mr. Weaver. He's delightfully smitten. Do not be surprised if he proposes tonight."

Tess's stomach clenched. No one would be proposing anything during a clandestine surveillance operation, thank

God, but she nodded to keep up the fiction. Ginny had proven herself both observant and shrewd, but even she didn't know about the orchids.

"Thank you for accompanying me on my walk," Tess said, for the benefit of anyone who might lurk within earshot. "With such a large gathering, I am in desperate need of a few moments of quiet."

"You're most welcome."

The two women continued toward the exit, entirely ignored by guests and servants alike. As they passed the parlor, Tess glanced inside. Jack's camera stood in its usual location, prepared for the morning photograph that could make him a star. She still didn't know how he intended to do it, but she was oddly nervous for him. She wanted him to win.

Her nose twitched. Her head swiveled automatically toward the source of the odor.

"Oh, no!"

"Is that smoke?" Ginny wondered.

Tess's feet began to move before her brain even processed the decision, carrying her toward the darkroom. She pulled the door open, waving away the smoke that wafted from the doorway. In one corner of the room, flames two feet high licked at the walls. She covered her mouth and nose against the stench of the burning chemicals.

"Get the camera!" she shouted to Ginny. "Call for help!"

Tess took a deep breath and plunged into the darkroom.

"Tess, no!"

"Get the camera!" Tess shouted again. She had to do whatever she could. The fire was growing by the second. Five minutes more and everything Jack had worked for would be burnt to ash.

She grabbed a plate holder, tucking it under her arm as she raced for the corner and sent up a prayer of thanks she'd spent so much time snooping around the room. She snagged the box with all of Jack's prints, plunking it and the plate holder atop the crate that held the negatives.

The crate was too heavy to lift, so she grabbed one handle and dragged it toward the door. The fire spread across the worktable, flickering its grimly beautiful dance of destruction. She could save nothing more. Only what was irreplaceable. Tess tugged and pulled, dragging the box of glass plates away from the heat and flames. Her eyes watered and she coughed. Sweat beaded on her skin. A portion of the worktable collapsed, sending sparks flying.

Tess cried out and yanked on the crate with all her might, hauling it through the doorway into the safer, cooler air of the parlor. A commotion had already arisen, with people rushing past and cries of, "Fire!" ringing through the halls.

"Tess, hurry, we must get out," Ginny urged. Jack's camera was in her arms, tripod and all.

Tess continued lugging the crate of negatives, determined to get it out of the house. "Fire!" she shouted, though her warning was now redundant. "Evacuate the castle!"

"You there!" Ginny called to a passing servant. "Help the lady with that box. Get it out of the house."

The burly man nudged Tess away from the crate and lifted it with shocking ease. "The nearest exit is this way, ladies. Please come quickly, but do not panic."

The moment Tess stepped outside into the cool night air, her pounding heart began to slow. The household had been alerted in time. Everyone would be safe. Much of Jack's equipment would be destroyed, but the camera was unharmed, and she had rescued the photos. He wouldn't be entirely ruined. His chances to win the five thousand, however, had dimmed considerably.

The last of her fear subsided, supplanted by a growing anger. Rowland. The bastard had sabotaged Jack to win the money for himself. Even without evidence, she knew it for the truth.

"Money," she growled. "It's always about the damned money. Not a thought for the people who are stepped on."

Her heart sank. This was why she couldn't contemplate a future with Jack. Knowing his history, she absolutely understood his reasons, but he still used people in his quest for financial security.

As if you are a pure altruist? a voice in the back of her mind nagged her. She'd used a falsified reference to save herself after her scandal. She lied her way into events to report on them. She'd intended to ruin a half-dozen spiritualists for her story and still intended to ruin Bardrick.

No, she was no better. Worse, perhaps, because she was a hypocrite as well. Maybe *he* was too good for *her*.

"Or maybe I don't know anything, anymore." Her heart was imagining photographic and journalistic collaborations and blue-eyed children. Her head was telling her to go back to her life of rules and order. For all her truth-seeking, Tess couldn't decide which one of them was the liar.

A gentle hand on her arm reminded Tess that Ginny was still with her. "Are you worried about Mr. Weaver? I thought you said he'd already gone outside?"

"Yes." He was likely waiting for her at the rendezvous point with no idea what had happened. "I should find him. Could you watch his equipment for me?"

"Of course. I'm happy to help in any way."

Tess nodded her thanks and hurried off, the box of photos still in her hands.

Word of the fire had spread quickly. The exit Tess and Ginny had taken was on a different side of the castle from the exit nearest the Great Hall, but the commotion of the mass exodus was loud enough to reach their ears. As Tess circled the castle, the noise grew louder, though no more intelligible. Shadowy figures in the distance raced through the gardens, streaming out of the castle into the restless night.

Tess clutched the small box of photographs. She had to find

Jack. She had to tell him what had happened. Perhaps in the chaos she would be able to slip away to the beach, unnoticed.

"This way, miss," a stern voice said to her. "His lordship wants everyone gathered a safe distance away."

"I'm looking for someone. Please excuse me."

She tried to walk past him, but he barred her way. "I'm afraid I must insist, miss."

Tess spun and started back the way she'd come. If no one would let her past, she'd go the long way around the castle.

"Tess! Miss Cochran!" Lydia's voice brought Tess to a halt.

"Ly— Madame Xyla," Tess replied, turning around once again. "I'm so glad to see you safe."

"And I, you. Jack is in a panic because he doesn't know where you are. Please, come with me."

"Thank you." Tess rushed off with Lydia, in the direction the stubborn man had insisted upon. They jogged through the gardens, out to the road, where Tess spied the figure of a man sitting on the ground, two others towering over him.

"Jack?" she called.

His head whipped around. "Tess!" He leapt to his feet and ran to her, stopping just shy of embracing her. Phantom mewled in his arms. "Thank God. I was so worried." His voice was raw and tight with pain. Moonlight glinted off tear-stained cheeks.

He knew. He knew about the fire and thought all was lost. Tess's heart broke for him.

She thrust out the box of photographs. "I saved your photos. The camera, too, and the negatives. I couldn't risk more, but you're not totally ruined. I'm so sorry this happened to you."

His jaw hung open. "You saved my camera? And my—" He gently set Phantom down, then reached out to trail his fingers lovingly across the box of photos, leaving it in Tess's hands. "My God. You... you..." He jerked back. "Are you out of your bloody mind? You could have been killed!"

"Excuse me?" Tess bristled. "I just saved your career and you're yelling at me?"

"My career is not worth your life!" Jack sank back down to the ground, putting his head in his hands. "Why? Why did you do it?"

Her burst of anger subsided. She knelt beside him, setting down the photos and lifting her skirts to keep the gown as clean as possible. "I was there, nearby, in time. I couldn't bear the thought of you out on the streets. Not when I could do something to help."

He reached for her hand. "You risked your life to help me. I'm not worth it, Tess."

"Yes you are. I'm sure Lydia agrees."

Tess looked up, but Lydia was walking away, shepherding the two big men who had been watching over Jack.

"Please don't ever do that again," Jack said.

"Please don't ever tell me what to do," Tess retorted.

"Dammit, Tess. I can't stand the thought of losing you."

"You've lost nothing," she insisted. "Or at least as little as possible."

"Thanks to you." He climbed back to his feet and held out a hand to help her up. "Please get up. I don't want to see your gorgeous dress ruined."

Tess took his hand, and when he pulled her into an embrace, she didn't resist, despite the crowd of people not far off. Phantom wound her way around their legs, purring.

"You've lost, though," Jack murmured. "You've missed your chance to sneak away to the beach. You're missing out on your orchid story. All for me. You are my heroine, Tess Cochran. I don't deserve you."

"I think you do." Her heart skipped a beat. Maybe he wasn't all wrong for her. Maybe he was exactly what she'd needed all along.

"No," he murmured. "I don't. But I will." He pressed a kiss to her cheek and then released her. "I won't compromise you in front of all these people, much as I want to." He bent to pick up his box of photos, then held out his free hand. "But I will take a turn about the gardens with you, if you will have me."

Tess put her hand in his. "Yes. I think I will. I know we can no longer go all the way to the beach, but perhaps you might escort me in that general direction?"

"Anything for you, love."

The intensity lurking beneath his flirtatious tone sent a shiver down her spine. This didn't have to end. The truth Tess had been seeking settled down into her soul. He was her path. She would find a way. She shivered again, from both the realization and the cold.

Jack shrugged out of his coat and draped it around her shoulders. He would keep her warm.

22

The Hierophant

"Feel free to lean on me if you're tired." Jack wrapped an arm around Tess's shoulders and pulled her across the library sofa until she was pressed tightly against him. "Or if you're not."

"I'm only going to rest my eyes for a moment," she replied.

"My thoughts exactly."

Jack let his head fall against hers, breathing deeply. A lingering hint of smoke mixed with the floral scent of the preparation she used on her hair. The smell of bravery. For him. Goddamn, he loved her. He would give her everything. All that he could. Even if "all" no longer included a trip around the world. He closed his eyes and held her.

A moment later, a shaft of sunlight and a sharp pain in his neck intruded on his rest. His eyes fluttered back open. Oh.

Well, that had been rather a longer moment than he intended. Several hours, judging by the encroaching daylight and the cramping of his muscles. He needed to move and stretch and work out the aches from too long sleeping in an awkward position.

But he had a happy kitten curled in his lap and a gorgeous woman tucked under his arm and they were all he wanted in the world. He didn't move.

"Morning, Jack," Tess sighed drowsily.

He moved a little.

Because his fingers were terribly close to the mound of one luscious breast swelling from the top of her bodice. He moved just enough to caress her satin-soft skin, tracing the plump, supple curve of her. Then, because he was a scoundrel, he moved further, letting his fingertips dip below the edge of her neckline. Because she was an adventuress, she twisted into his touch.

His questing fingers were pinching a pleasantly puckered nipple when a voice far too nearby said, "Did you hear the chatter about a ghost yacht?"

Jack yanked his hand away. Apparently he and Tess were no longer the only ones in the library.

"What nonsense," another voice replied. "I saw it with my own eyes. There was nothing ghostly about it."

Jack had to agree with that. He and Tess hadn't managed to walk all the way to the beach during those long hours before the castle had been declared safe enough for everyone to return inside, but they'd gotten close enough to get a good look at the boat. Tess had made a few notes. They'd been much too far to learn anything about the purchaser of the orchids, unfortunately, leaving a gaping hole in her story.

"All this haunting talk is such nonsense," the first voice said. "I can't imagine why anyone believes it, but it seems many of the people here do. Everyone was raving about those Tarot readings Madame Xyla was doing in the garden last night."

"Yes. And the spirit photography. The men are obsessed with the spirit photography. Lord Haverstock told me Lord Bardrick has sent an urgent summons to bring in another photographer so he can hold his final portrait session."

Jack's whole body jerked, startling Phantom, who leapt from his lap with an unhappy meow. A new photographer to replace him? Like hell!

He wiggled his way out from Tess's embrace, brushing his lips across her cheek. "Have to go to work, darling. Busy day ahead. Wish I could spend it all with you."

I wish I could spend forever with you.

He forced himself to his feet. He wanted to hold her, wanted to make love to her, wanted it all so badly it hurt. But he had to be a man worthy of her, and the only way to do that was to make certain she walked out of this castle with the story of a lifetime. Whatever it took. Whatever it cost.

Jack bent to whisper in her ear. "When the time comes, I want you to denounce me. Loudly. Be Tess the Truth-seeker for me."

"Jack…" she began, but he couldn't allow her husky voice to distract him. He had plans. He blew her a kiss as he hurried for the door.

Three hours later, Jack stood in the Great Hall, his camera set to capture the best light and a ridiculous crowd pressing in on him. He'd had to spend most of his winnings from his card games to pay for the use of equipment and chemicals belonging to the emergency photographer. He'd paid at least ten times the actual cost of the materials he was using, but what choice did he have? He wasn't going to let Rowland beat him, and he intended to ensure Tess left this party with a story to tell.

"Why is it so indistinct?" Bardrick demanded of the new photographer, scowling at the print he had finished only moments before.

"Spirits are capricious," the photographer explained. "They are difficult to capture even for a moment, and one particularly summoned may not wish…"

"No, no, you've obviously done something wrong. Where's that Weaver lad? Is he ready yet?"

"Right here, your lordship," Jack called, waving a hand to catch the earl's attention above the crowd. "I am absolutely ready. But are you? You will wish to be in a state of relaxation and comfort for the best results. You aren't feeling any lingering apprehension from the events of last night, I hope?"

The clenching of Bardrick's jaw said he very much was. Which didn't surprise Jack in the least. Dozens of people had seen the smuggler's boat and were speculating on what it was. Many guests doubted the rumors of hauntings, and a portion of the castle would be unusable for several months. Bardrick's cover-up for his crimes had suffered a serious blow, and he was desperate to repair the damage. All he had left to convince the world that the only intrigue in the castle was of the ghostly kind were the prize money and his word. Fail, and more people than just Tess would go digging for the truth. The orchid scheme would crumble.

Jack did his best not to let his satisfaction show.

"Yes, yes, I am perfectly well," Bardrick growled. "A minor difficulty. Nothing a stout heart can't handle." His gaze darted toward Rowland, burning for a moment in fury before he composed himself. It seemed Jack and Bardrick genuinely agreed on something, for once.

"If you could stand just over here, where the camera is pointed," Jack said, waving Bardrick into position. "Yes. A bit to the right." Jack peered through the camera to adjust the focus. "One more step, please. There. Perfect."

In a different location than his original plan for the shot, Jack couldn't be one hundred percent certain about Bardrick's placement, but his puffed-up standing pose with both hands grasping his lapels would compensate for any small errors. No hands reaching out for spirits or sofas where seated figures needed to appear side-by-side. The simpler, the better.

Jack took only a single exposure, then ducked into the small, awkward tent serving as a darkroom for the day. Working in the cramped quarters slowed him down, but the wait would give the crowd more time to chatter. Anticipation was good. He'd primed Sir Cyril and Lord Haverstock earlier, reminding them of all the previous photos and how marvelous they'd all been. They would be stirring up interest, he hoped.

Jack grinned at the completed negative. No one in the castle would see this coming. He readied the paper to make a print, and stepped back out into the light to expose it, along with a special "test photo" he'd made earlier from some of the precious negatives Tess had saved. When both were completed, he paused a moment to examine them alone, admiring his handiwork. Some of his best. He returned all the equipment to the darkroom, tucked his special photo away, and rejoined the crowd to present Bardrick's final spirit image.

"Well, boy, how is it?" the earl demanded.

"Excellent. An astonishing result." Jack handed over the photo.

Bardrick's eyes swept over the photo, taking in his imperious pose and the ghostly creature beside him. Furry and black, with a small white patch near her right ear, Phantom's phantom form sat regally as a queen. Tiny, but no less proud than the aristocrat beside her.

Blood drained from Bardrick's face. His fingers clenched on the paper. He opened his mouth to bellow as guests crowded around him, all of them desperate for a glimpse of the summoned spirit.

Jack sucked in a breath. Everything rested on Bardrick pretending to believe.

Right on cue, voices began to ring out.

"How extraordinary!" Lydia.

"What a marvel!" Lady Virginia.

"A cat? What rubbish!" Rowland, naturally. Jack had anticipated such a reaction and the bastard hadn't disappointed.

The murmur spread through the crowd. *A cat? A ghost cat? Who summons a cat?*

"Deuced brilliant, Bardrick!" Sir Cyril exclaimed. "We'd been expecting some figure from history. Julius Caesar. William of Normandy. Her Majesty's beloved Prince Albert. But this is *proof!* No one could have guessed."

Jack's cheeks hurt from holding back his smile. God love Sir Cyril Montague. Jack would be sending him and his wife an illustrated book of naughty poetry as thanks.

Someone had grabbed the photograph, and it circulated through the crowd to gasps of astonishment and delight.

"Spectacular!"

"Very fine, indeed!"

"How did you do it?" Haverstock asked. "I can't even get a live animal to respond to my commands. And certainly not a cat. Ornery beasts, they are. You must be dam— dashed powerful."

"I say!" another voice broke in. "Is that the creature that's been screeching at night? I knew this place was haunted!"

"The ghostly noises have persisted for years," Bardrick said, fully recovered now that he had an opportunity to substantiate his rumors. "Some say the sounds are the cries of the crew of the yacht that foundered offshore, taking the Ninth Earl of Bardrick with it. My ancestor gave his life in pursuit of the smugglers who plagued these shores."

Jack smirked. *Your ancestor was a smuggler himself and you've taken up his legacy.*

"I saw that ghost boat last night!" a man shouted.

"I saw the cat," a woman added. "There and then gone. Exactly the image in the photo."

"Bonaparte," Bardrick explained. "My boyhood companion, until he used all nine of his lives. He's walked the castle grounds ever since."

The crowd was in agreement. The castle was truly haunted. The ghost cat was proof. Bardrick's talent for contacting the spirit world was unrivaled. The more they gushed, the taller Bardrick stood. Rowland scowled silently, too afraid of his employer's censure to complain.

Jack looked to Tess, catching her eye and giving her a nod. The circulating photograph was only a few hands away from her. She shook her head.

Do it, Jack pleaded silently. *Take your story. Denounce me.*

The man beside her handed over the photograph and she studied it for a moment. A smile tugged at the corners of her lips. She recognized Phantom. She admired Jack's efforts. Her eyes lifted once again, meeting Jack's.

Trust me, he mouthed.

"Oh, for heaven's sake!" Tess exclaimed.

Jack's heart soared. Brilliant, magnificent Tess. He doubted she knew why he'd asked her to denounce him, but she stood tall, the photograph in her hand, ready to do it. Trusting a scoundrel.

"There is no ghost cat," she said in a voice full of certainty.

His heart hammered in his chest. He was going to miss her. Dear God, was he going to miss her. Maybe someday. Maybe when he'd made something of himself, he could find her and beg for a chance. For now, he stared at her, trying to imprint her bold and beautiful image onto his brain for all eternity.

He wasn't the only one staring. Heads around the room turned to gape at the young woman who dared to call Jack—and with him Bardrick—a liar.

"It's the perfectly ordinary cat who lives in the conservatory," Tess scoffed. "This." She waved the photograph. "Isn't even a good trick. It's a simple double exposure. Take a photo of a cat, then use the same unwashed glass plate to take the photo of Lord Bardrick."

"Ha! I knew it!" Rowland, now emboldened, jabbed a finger at Jack. "It's true, isn't it, Weaver?"

"No, it isn't," Jack replied, cheerfully truthful. He'd simply reused photo paper with a faint image of Phantom already printed on it. With no one watching him, the straightforward process had sufficed.

"Of course it's not true," Bardrick snarled. "The hauntings are real, and *I* have proven it. With the help of a fine camera."

But the damage was done. Tess's words had given other skeptics the courage to speak up. All throughout the room, voices rose in agreement. Somewhere in the back, laughter broke out, spreading through the guests until the whole hall echoed with the sound of snickering.

Rowland stalked toward Jack, eyes alight with malevolent triumph. Jack took several steps backward. "This man," Rowland declared, "is nothing but a swindler!"

"I am much, much more than a swindler," Jack replied softly. For the first time in many years, he actually believed it.

"Shut your mouth, you knave!" Bardrick yelled at his former lackey. "How dare you slander me with such lies! Be gone!"

Rowland's face turned red with fury. He could vilify Jack all he wanted, but he'd still lost. "Slander you? You're a swindler too! The worst of the lot!" He turned to the crowd. "Bardrick sells fake orchids! Cuts them up himself in his conservatory! He's a fraud and a thief!"

"Get him out of here!" Bardrick roared.

Half a dozen servants shoved through the crowd to seize Rowland. They dragged him away, his howls as shrill as Phantom's had ever been.

The entire party had fallen silent. Jack scanned their faces, picking out which guests were confused, which fascinated, and which hungover from all they'd drunk during the night. He slowly worked his way back toward the camera and the darkroom, concealing himself in the mass of humanity.

"Is it true about the orchids?" a voice called out.

Bardrick flinched, but then cleared his throat. "That man is insane. Madly jealous of my ability to grow perfectly ordinary orchids as a hobby, while he struggles to do the same. There will be no more such nonsense. Now follow me, please, as I lead the party on a tour of my haunted castle."

"Show us the orchids!"

"Let's see the conservatory!"

"Of course we will see the conservatory," Bardrick exclaimed, his voice unnaturally cheery. "It shall be the *final* stop on our grand tour. First, the north tower. The most haunted place in the castle."

The assembly began to move. Jack dashed into the darkroom. He had one more photograph to take, and no time to lose.

23

The Hanged Man

JACK SWORE TO HIMSELF this was absolutely the last time he would ever crawl through a conservatory on his hands and knees. In fact, he would give serious consideration to never entering a conservatory ever again after today. Surely his presence here made him a candidate for Bedlam. He squirmed across the floor, his right arm aching from holding the camera securely. He'd barely had time to take one hopefully adequate photo before Bardrick's two smuggling cronies had burst in to conceal the evidence of orchid tampering.

Almost there. He had to get out. If he didn't get back to the darkroom in time and get the photo developed before the plate dried, Tess would have no photograph for her story. And if the rest of the party arrived before he escaped, he'd be discovered for sure.

Phantom had found him, of course, and butted her head against his arm repeatedly, wanting to cuddle or play.

Not now, girl. I...

He froze as the idea came to him. If he could get her howling, it would cover the sounds of his departure. He pulled his pocket watch out, unclipped it from his waistcoat and dangled it like a toy for the kitten. Phantom batted at it.

Good girl.

He swung it slowly, then faster and in larger circles, encouraging her to jump and pounce.

That's it. Now for your big moment. Go get it for me!

He flung the watch behind him and she scampered after

it, making the closest sound to a mighty roar he'd ever heard from a little cat. Jack leapt to his feet and dashed out the door.

He didn't pause for even a moment. He streaked down the halls, dodging the tired, overworked servants who were trying to keep the house in some order during these last few hours of the party. He called out apologies but didn't slow down.

In the darkroom at last, he poured the developer with hands still shaky from the ordeal. This photograph would be nowhere near his best, but he hoped it would suffice. The final print came out clearly, the workbench with its orchid-altering tools sharply in focus, even if the edges of the photo were uneven and blurred. Good enough. Jack gathered his things and hurried up to his bedchamber.

His camera went into the center of his trunk, his clothing stuffed all around it. He no longer cared if his suits were kept neat and tidy. All that mattered was that the camera survived the journey intact. His few valuables, his little remaining money, and the most important photos he placed in his personal satchel, slinging it across his body. If another disaster befell him and his luggage was lost or destroyed, he would have those, at least.

Jack pulled the bell cord to ring for a servant and sat down to write.

His pen shook. He wanted to pour out his heart to Tess and ramble on and on about how much he loved her. Absurd. She cared for him, certainly, but how deep her feelings went, he didn't know. She'd never said what was in her own heart. He could only speculate and hope she felt the way he did.

Or was that selfish? Surely it would be better for her to move on and forget him entirely.

That thought was morose enough to force him to concentrate on the important issue: giving her information that would make her articles shine.

The knock came just as he was finishing.

"I'd like my things taken downstairs and a carriage readied

to convey me to the train station," he told the man who had answered his summons. "I need to depart as soon as possible."

"Of course, sir. I'm sorry your business takes you away before the end of the party."

"So am I."

Jack watched his possessions disappear down the hall, then slipped into Tess's room to leave the letter and photographs for her. Memories of their night together here filled his chest with a bittersweet ache. He dug his pen from his bag and scribbled a hasty postscript at the bottom of the note.

"Goodbye, love," he whispered, then stepped back into the hall.

A small black furball marched proudly down the corridor toward him, a gold pocketwatch dangling from her teeth. Maybe Phantom *was* part ghost. She seemed to have a supernatural talent for finding him. She deposited the watch at his feet.

"Why, thank you." He picked up the watch, laughing at the little teeth and claw marks left by her hunt. He'd never be able to sell the watch, but now he'd never want to. "I think it's fate, girl. You and I are meant to be." He scooped up the cat and tucked her into the bag. She poked her head out the top and purred.

Jack scratched Phantom behind the ears and started for the exit, not looking back. "I only wish it were three of us."

⁓

Tess jabbed a toe at the unusual gap between the tiles in the conservatory floor beneath the workbench. Invisible in the darkness, and subtle even with sunlight streaming through the glass ceiling, she'd only spotted it because she'd been looking for exactly such a thing. Another hidden door, like in the wine cellar. She doubted this one led to anything more than a small storage area. A good place for Bardrick to hide his tools. His men had done well stashing everything away.

A few remaining modified orchids sat inside a pair of Wardian cases, obscured behind hazy glass. Despite the fire, the ghost yacht must have sailed off with hundreds of altered specimens, given the huge empty area in the rear of the conservatory.

"I call these 'ghost orchids,'" Bardrick announced to the crowd.

Appreciative murmurs spread around the room. The attitude of the party had shifted after Jack's wild photo session. No one cared any longer whether the hauntings were real or whether Rowland's accusations were true. They wanted only spectacle, of any variety. Bardrick clung stubbornly to the remnants of his pride, refusing to admit any mistake or error in judgement.

Jack had been right about that. Tess had been certain denouncing him would ruin everything. She'd tried to talk to him during their brief interactions that morning, but he'd said only, "Trust me," and, "It will help your story." She'd hesitated to do it, until the moment came and everyone had been acting so *stupid*. Everyone but Jack and his absurdly audacious photograph. He'd asked her for the truth and she'd given it.

"These orchids are not rare," Bardrick explained to an enthusiastic segment of the group, "but they have been specially cultivated to grow well in an English hothouse. They are worth enough that I cannot give them away to fellow enthusiasts. I can, however, part with select samples for their base value."

He departed the conservatory many hundred pounds wealthier and fifty orchids shorter. Tess almost stole a small specimen on her way out, for no other reason than to be defiant. Jack Weaver was apparently a terrible influence. Or perhaps he'd only made her reassess what mattered to her.

And where was he? He'd vanished after the photo uproar and she hadn't seen him since. Surely he would appear for the announcement of the prize winner?

Tess stayed to the rear of the crowd as they all strolled

into the ballroom, then took up her customary place along the wall. No sign of him. Her stomach began to churn. Something was wrong.

Every moment he didn't appear compounded her agitation. Her shoulders tensed. Her fingers curled. Terrible scenarios began to race through her mind, from death by potassium cyanide in the darkroom to further sabotage from Rowland.

"Where is my photographer?" Bardrick demanded. "I can't very well award him a prize if he's not here."

Lydia stepped up, drawing back her veil to give Bardrick a good look at her unusually-colored eyes. "I would be happy to accept the prize on my cousin's behalf."

A new set of whispers traveled through the assembly. Madame Xyla and Jack Weaver, family? Did they come from a long line of spiritualists? Perhaps they were not cousins, but twins, and the natural magnetism between them heightened their metaphysical senses.

Oh, for God's sake.

Tess headed for the door. She wasn't in the mood to listen to ludicrous, small-minded, or otherwise annoying comments. Lydia could negotiate with Bardrick on her own. Tess intended to find Jack.

The Great Hall was empty, the portable darkroom dismantled. A quick look into the library found it likewise deserted. Tess trudged upstairs, but hammering on Jack's door brought no answer.

She stood in the hall, tapping her toe irritably as she contemplated other options. Could she sneak into the closed-off, fire-damaged section of the castle? She wouldn't be terribly surprised to find Jack had gone to search the wreckage for anything possibly salvageable. But why not invite her along? He loved to encourage her adventures. No, there was more to this absence than roaming the castle without her. Tess pulled out her key and slipped into her room to think.

A pile of papers sat on the table awaiting her.

"Goddammit, Jack!"

She sank heavily into a chair, unable to muster the will to open the letter or peruse the photographs. She already knew what this meant. He'd left. He'd left her and any hope of the five thousand pounds for some stupid, foolish, chivalrous reason. Tears welled in her eyes. The rational voice had been right after all. They weren't meant to be.

Tess swiped at her eyes. Too little sleep had left her overly emotional, that was all. She needed to do the sensible thing and read the letter.

My dearest Tess,

Please forgive my sudden departure, but given the circumstances, I believe it best to begin preparations for my next endeavor as promptly as possible. I have herein enclosed information which I hope will be of value to you as you write your articles, including my observations from the conservatory this morning, a variety of tricks which can be used in the production of a spirit photograph, and a number of photographs which will support your articles. Please do not hesitate to use any and all of them. I ask only that you do not include Lydia in any of your exposés, that she may continue to ply her trade unmolested. I wish you the very best life possible. Please seek any and all happiness wherever and with whomever you may desire.

Tess swore again. She hadn't needed to expose him. The orchid story would be plenty titillating. She flipped through the photos. One of the conservatory, showing the orchids and tools for altering them. A number of copies of Bardrick's spirit images, including the final photo starring Phantom as a phantom.

Her hand froze on the bottom image. There she stood, as she had looked the night they'd met at Madame Xyla's seance. Beside her, a ghostly figure of a man, indistinct but for a crystal-clear pair of eyes, one of which bore a small, dark patch.

Common Methods of Production of Spirit Photographs:
1) *reuse glass plate without fully cleaning off old image*
2) *reflect ghostly image into lens during exposure*
3) *have accomplice swathed in white pose briefly behind the sitter*
4) *hide glass plate with spirit image inside camera to imprint secondary image onto final plate*
5) *place spirit image behind exposed plate while still sensitive, then re-expose*
6) *print spirit photo on paper, then reuse same paper to print final image*

Guess which one(s) I used to create the photo of you and I. (Hint: I used your original negative.)

"Why would you do such a thing?" Tess lamented. She didn't need him to answer. She knew. Because he loved her. He loved her and wouldn't allow anything to endanger her career and the life she'd crafted for herself. Even him. "Well, maybe you don't know everything, Jack Weaver. Maybe I'm done being Tess the Scared of Scandal. Maybe now I'm only Tess Who Lives for Adventure."

She looked down at the postscript scrawled at the bottom of the letter.

I recant my earlier statement. I love you and selfishly want you for my own. I've gone to seek my fortune, but will search for you when I can afford to marry. Please, please wait for me.

-Jack

Tess gathered up the papers and began to pack her bags. Work called.

24

Justice

The Earl's New Scandal

*O*UR READERS HAVE NO DOUBT HEARD *the news coming lately from Bardrick Castle: first the £5000 prize offered to the spiritualist who could prove the castle haunted, and then the fire interrupting the lavish party. Rumors, too, have no doubt reached your ears.*

I, dear readers, am here to give you the truth. The truth of the spiritualists. The truth of the fire. The truth of the rumors of ghosts and cats, orchids and yachts. I have a talent, you see, for observing what others might miss, and whenever I attend an event, I always have my pen at the ready.

Among the spiritualists invited to compete was a young photographer named Jack Weaver. He was a swindler, I was certain, there to claim the prize through fraudulent methods. Imagine my surprise, only days into the two-week-long event, when I found myself assisting this spirit photographer to expose something entirely different than photographs…

…The photograph here, provided by Mr. Weaver, testifies to the truth of the scandalous goings-on he and I uncovered in our investigations. Other photographs from the event, including the falsified spirit images, have been provided to the newspaper and may be printed at their discretion.

> *It is the considered opinion of this journalist that though the spirit photographs Mr. Weaver provided for the Earl were created deliberately to cause distraction and aid in his investigation—by means known to any photographer of talent—his creation of them was so skillful he fully deserved the prize which he graciously opted to decline.*
>
> *As for the spirit photographs he produces on a regular basis, this reporter witnessed the production of many such photos and observed nothing that might testify against their authenticity. I invite readers to draw their own conclusions on the matter, and assert that no matter what style of photograph you are seeking, you could not go wrong seeking out his services.*
>
> -Miss T. Cochran

One week later

Tess barged into the meeting of the newly formed Independent Ladies' Suffrage Association without waiting for a proper announcement from Ginny's butler. The four current members of the club looked up from their tea. Ginny's face broke into a broad grin.

"Miss Cochran! Welcome! We were just discussing your article. Have you reconsidered my invitation and decided to join us?"

Tess shook her head. She accepted the seat her hostess indicated and poured herself a cup of tea. "I'm afraid not. I've actually come to say goodbye. I will be sailing for America shortly."

Lydia set her cup in its saucer. Her short blond curls and pale blue dress made a stark contrast to the vivid colors and dark wig she adopted as Madame Xyla. Tess was pleased to see her here, in this space where she was free from any need to perform.

"So that's what my cousin is up to," Lydia said. "The stubborn man. He's answered none of my messages."

"Nor mine," Tess sighed. "His apartment has been emptied, and all my inquiries suggest he's sold almost all his possessions to buy transport to Liverpool and passage on a ship to New York. I'm convinced he didn't actually read my article."

"But we all did!" Ginny waved a newspaper clipping. "It's part of today's discussion of available occupations for women. You have made it abundantly clear that journalistic investigator is one of them."

"Thank you," Tess replied. "I'm sorry it comes at a time when I'm abandoning said occupation to chase down a man."

Ginny made a dismissive gesture. "Bah! If you thought for a moment you couldn't support yourself with your talents and your savings, you wouldn't be walking away from your career. You have grand plans, I imagine. Plans that allow you to go after your love and drag him home."

Tess couldn't help but smile, thinking of her imagined future. It was a risk. It was an adventure. But it was all that she wanted.

"Actually, I don't intend to drag him anywhere. I will go wherever he does. The more places the better. Travel guidebooks are all the rage, and I intend to pen one specifically for women. Scandal is everywhere, and I can always sell gossip stories to make ends meet, but once word spreads that 'T. Cochran' is a woman, I believe ladies will scramble to buy my guide. And to make it sparkle, I need my photographer."

Ginny grabbed for a piece of paper and a pen. "Guidebook author. We shall add that to the list. I will buy multiple copies of your book, I'm sure. And you must become a member of the club. Our remote agent. You can connect us with women's rights groups around the world."

"I doubt I'll be seeing any of the world outside America. I anticipate second- and third-class travel by stage and train as

Jack attempts to 'make his fortune' or whatever mad scheme he has in his head."

Lydia's blond curls bounced as she shook her head. "Nonsense. You'll have plenty of money to travel in style to any part of the world you desire. I'm now a very wealthy woman, remember, and you may inform my cousin that, as soon as he answers my letters, I will arrange for him to have the usual twenty percent."

Tess pursed her lips. "You think he will accept a thousand pounds, even after he forfeited his claim on the prize?"

"He doesn't have much choice. He earned the money and if he won't take it, I'll give it to him through you. 'The usual twenty percent.' Tell him exactly that."

"I will. And, Ginny, I would be delighted to be a member in remote of your lovely group."

"Excellent. All you must do to be a member in good standing is to support other women in their quest for independence and happiness and remember to always take your tea with a splash of defiance."

Tess laughed. Today an adventure called to her, but whenever she returned to London, she knew she would find friends waiting. "That I can do," she said. "And gladly."

25

The Sun

J ACK STARED OVER THE RAIL at the shrinking coastline, the queasiness in his stomach caused not by the motion of the steamship but by the loss of the only home he'd ever known.

Or is it only the loss of a certain woman? The loss of what might have been.

He jerked upright and began the long walk to the opposite end of the deck. Phantom trotted along beside him, peering curiously at everything, but reluctant to stray too far from his side.

He would look forward, not back. America would be good for him. He could roam from place to place until he found something he was good at that didn't involve scamming people. Perhaps if he set up a photographic studio in a mid-sized city where the competition would be minimal he could make a living as a portraitist. Earn enough to offer Tess a proper courtship.

He hoped her career would be getting a well-deserved boost from her recent article. He hadn't read it. In fact, he'd avoided anything at all connected with her for fear he might lose his resolve and go running to seek her out. Including Lydia's letters. He'd open them once he reached New York and write her a lengthy apology.

"Excuse me, sir?"

Jack turned toward the crewman who had spoken. "Yes?"

"Are you Mr. Jack Weaver?"

"I am." Jack eyed the man warily, trying to think if he'd

done anything while boarding that might possibly have caused trouble. He didn't see how he could have. He hadn't talked to anyone, too wrapped up in maudlin thoughts about the improbability of ever seeing Tess again. Maybe he wasn't supposed to have a cat running loose?

"Excellent. Glad to have found you, sir," the crewman went on. "I have come to apologize for the mixup with your ticket."

Jack blinked rapidly. *What the devil?*

"We are terribly sorry for the confusion and the inconvenience. I would like to assure you that after speaking with your wife, the matter has been corrected. Your trunks have been transported to your stateroom. I have your key here."

"My wife," Jack repeated, the words coming out oddly flat despite the pounding in his chest and butterflies dancing in his stomach.

"Everything of hers was in order and she asked us to inform you that she is resting in the cabin."

"Of course." Jack looked down at the key in his hand. *Cabin. Wife. Tess. Oh, God, Tess.* "Thank you."

"It's my pleasure, sir. Please enjoy the voyage."

"I… I might, at that." Jack's fingers tightened around the key and he jogged off in search of his surprise accommodations.

His hand shook and the key bumped against the lock before sliding into place. What in God's name was she doing here? Why would she abandon everything for him? That was crazy, right? His kind of crazy. Maybe they *were* meant to be.

Jack pushed open the door and stepped inside. Phantom darted past him, racing to Tess's side and meowing expectantly up at her.

Tess set down the brush she was running through her loose auburn locks and turned to pet Phantom, smiling, before lifting her head to look Jack in the eye.

"Hello, Jack. It's good to see you."

"Uh…" All his usual charisma deserted him. Tess sat at the dressing table, stripped down to her undergarments. Her peacock blue corset was embroidered with elegant swirls and trimmed with satin ribbon. Matching stockings hugged her legs. Her shift and drawers were a paler shade of blue, also trimmed with ribbon.

"Do you like my new things? I bought them for you."

"I want to photograph you, just like you are now," he blurted. *Smooth, Weaver. Why don't you add that you'd like to hang her on your wall and stroke yourself off to the sight of her?*

A smile cracked through his stupor. This was Tess. She'd probably like that.

"What are you thinking?" she asked.

"I'm imagining photographing you in many, many states of undress and papering the wall above my bed with your beauty."

"Hmmm." She rose from her seat, crossing the small cabin in a few quick strides. "This only seems fair if I get similar photos of you."

He reached for her, no longer caring why she was here or what he was going to do about it. He needed her, in his arms, right now. When their bodies collided they gasped as one.

"Take as many as you'd like, love," Jack murmured, and then his lips found hers.

He could have dwelt in that glorious kiss for all eternity. Tess was a gleaming ray of sunshine after a storm, the crackle of a warm fire in the cold, the place he could come home to no matter where in the world he might be.

Her hands dug into his clothing, holding him captive as her mouth claimed him, declaring what he ought to have known all along: he couldn't run. He was hers and she would come for him.

He ran his hand up and down her corset, delighting in her curves and the way she'd displayed them for his pleasure. He peeled away each layer with care, wanting to preserve every piece for future encounters.

Tess was nowhere near so fastidious. She yanked and tugged at his suit, baring him to her touch as swiftly as possible.

In no time she had him naked on the bed beneath her, grinding her hips against his, ready for their bodies to join.

"You didn't happen... to buy any... sheaths?" he gasped.

"No. Instead I've brought a willingness to have your children."

He could say nothing to that except to groan and grasp her tightly by the waist as she lowered herself onto him. She set her own pace, moving slowly at first, then faster and harder as she found her pleasure, and all he could do was thrust to the rhythm she set and hang on for dear life. When she moaned his name, trembling above him, she sent him over the edge, driven half to madness from the force of the climax.

Tess crumpled on top of him, her chest heaving, her brow damp with sweat and her lips tilted up in a smile of satisfied exhaustion. "See what you almost missed out on by running from me?"

"You make a compelling argument, beautiful." Jack twisted a strand of her hair around a finger while his other hand brushed gentle caresses along her spine. "And I haven't forgotten that hairpin I owe you. I *will* buy you one someday."

Tess turned to press her cheek to his shoulder, emitting a contented sigh. "Only you would remember such a silly thing." Her fingers trailed across his chest. "I love you, Jack Weaver."

"Terrible judgement on your part, I'm afraid," he teased.

She poked him. "No, it's not. You're always underestimating yourself."

"Why did you come for me? I have nothing to offer you. No money, no job, no useful skills."

"Do you even hear yourself? You're talking nonsense. You're a brilliant photographer and a natural salesman. That's a career, right there. Besides, I don't need your money. I have skills of my own."

"Very true. But won't being associated with a known conman hurt your reputation?"

Tess sat partway up and frowned down at him. "You didn't read my article, did you?"

"No."

"And I don't imagine you read Lydia's letters?"

"That would also be a 'no.'"

"Well, she was granted the five thousand pound prize and she says she intends to give you, 'the usual twenty percent.' You can open your studio anywhere in the world with a fortune of one thousand pounds."

"Twenty-five hundred," Jack corrected.

"What?"

"She intends to give me half. It's what we've always done. Negotiate a deal for twenty percent, then give the other person half. But I can't accept it. If I'm going to be the man you deserve, I have to make something of myself."

"You already have done. A true scoundrel would've taken the money, not run from it. You don't have to prove anything, Jack. You've already shown me your true character. So why not sail around the world with me? This is our chance for adventure and our chance to make our living doing the things we love. Why not take it?"

He hugged her and kissed her cheek. "You win. I'm not that altruistic."

"Neither am I. We're seeing the world, and I'm going to write about it and you're going to photograph it."

"Yes, ma'am." He kissed her again, on the lips, taking his time to savor and adore her. "I love you, Tess Cochran."

"It's Tess Weaver now."

Jack chuckled. "Ah, yes. Another grave miscalculation of yours."

"How so?"

"Well, you've stolen my name, and I'm not going to take it back."

"Hmmm..." Tess's fingers began to wander across his

chest, igniting a new burst of desire. "I suppose I'll simply have to marry you for real."

"I suppose you will."

He sank into another kiss, swept out to sea on a wave of love and joy. Whatever shore they washed up upon, he knew they'd be together. Adventure awaited.

Epilogue
The World

Boston, Massachusetts
Four years later

"Thank you, Mr. Weaver," said the teary-eyed man clutching a photo with the spirit image of his late wife. "It means so much to me to see her again."

"It was my pleasure, sir," Jack replied truthfully. "If I can reconnect people, even for an instant, I know I have done something right."

He escorted the satisfied client to the door, watching the man walk away beyond the painted letters that advertised the studio to all passers-by.

Jack Weaver - Portraits and Specialized Photography

A nice, polite way to say he'd photograph almost anything. His travel photos had been widely published, but spirit photos continued to be one of his biggest sources of income, second only to the low-cost tintype portraits of individuals and families. Occasionally he shot bizarre trick photos or scandalous nudes, but those commissions were rare.

"Papa!"

A tiny hand tugged on his trousers, urging him away from the door.

"What is it, Alex?"

Alexandria looked up at him with eyes that matched his own. Her auburn hair fell in untidy waves, framing her round face. She reached for his hand and led him into the next room, where she walked him to a chair and pushed him into it.

"Sit," she commanded.

Jack watched in amusement as she pretended to pour from an empty bottle onto a battered tin plate. She jammed the plate into the back of the old camera that had become her toy, then removed the lens cap. It was the most adorable thing he'd ever seen.

He watched her play for a full half-hour, letting her pose him in various ways. He made a much more manageable client than Phantom, who would only pose when and where she liked, unless enticed with bits of meat.

Alex had just begun to tire of the game and Jack was considering putting her down for a nap, when the bell above the front door jingled. He hopped up from his seat and scooped his daughter into his arms. His next session wasn't scheduled until the top of the hour, which meant the noise could only be one person.

"Mama!" Alexandria shrieked in delight, wriggling until Jack set her down and let her race across the room to Tess.

He followed right on her heels. Three days apart was three too many.

They all crashed together in an awkward family embrace. Even Phantom joined in, rubbing up against Tess's skirts until Tess picked her up and petted her. Jack barely squeezed in a kiss.

"More later," he whispered. He stepped back and took up her bag. "How was your trip?"

A smashing success, if the grin stretching ear-to-ear said anything. "The new *Families' Travel Guide to the 38 States* was well-received. I've been asked to do a European tour to write the next in the series as well as the next *Ladies' Travel Guide*." She bounced in place. "Two books!"

"Congratulations, love."

"Mama, mama!" Alex tugged on Tess's skirts. "Come sit!"

Jack leaned close to his wife. "Be prepared to swoon from the adorableness. I almost had to call for a vinaigrette."

Tess rolled her eyes, but soon she too had fallen under Alexandria's spell and was lounging in pose after pose, trying not to laugh or interrupt with impromptu hugs. Sadly, Jack had to abandon the new round of toddler photography for his next client. By the time he'd finished, she was down for a nap and he had a moment to spend alone with Tess.

They slipped together into their bedroom, properly greeting one another at last with a long, hungry kiss.

"Do you have any other clients today?" she asked.

"No. I was going to do some experimenting, but I can put that off."

"Good, then put off your clothing as well and give me another kiss."

That he could certainly do. They scrambled into bed and before long they were lying spent and satisfied in one another's arms.

"So, Europe?" he asked, trailing a finger down between her breasts. "I like the sound of that. Plenty of good names there for our next child. Valencia, Paris, Hamburg."

She poked him. "I intend to begin with a long visit with Lydia and Ginny, so we might end up with a London."

"Hmm. We'd better take precautions on the ship. Atlantic Ocean is a bit of a mouthful."

"This is why I have the final say over all names."

He kissed her bare shoulder. "You thought up Alex's name in the first place. You are just as bad as I am. You simply are less likely to admit it."

Her lips quirked in a half-smile. "Perhaps. When can we leave?"

"I have sessions scheduled for the next two weeks. After that, I'm free to depart whenever you desire."

"Perfect. I'll make the arrangements. I should warn you that during some of our travels I will have to sit apart from you and pretend not to know you. I need to get both the family perspective and the single woman perspective."

"Not know me? You're such a liar," he teased.

"You would know, darling."

"Sadly true. But this is excellent. I'll have an opportunity to be the devilish stranger who flirts with you. I will use my adorable daughter and cat to lure you in. And then I'll seduce you."

"Now *there's* a truth for you."

Jack laughed. "Indeed. And here's another one." He turned to take her fully into his arms. "I love you. Wherever we go, you're the best adventure a man could ever have."

And with that, he kissed her again.

Maybe the next child would be named Boston.

The End

About the Author

AWARD-WINNING AUTHOR CATHERINE STEIN believes that everyone deserves love and that Happily Ever After has the power to help, to heal, and to comfort. She writes sassy, sexy romance set during the Victorian and Edwardian eras. Her stories are full of action, adventure, magic, and fantastic technologies.

Catherine lives in Michigan with her husband and three rambunctious girls. She loves steampunk and Oxford commas, and can often be found dressed in Renaissance festival clothing, drinking copious amounts of tea.

Visit Catherine online at
www.catsteinbooks.com
and join her VIP mailing list for a free short story.

Follow her on Twitter @catsteinbooks,
or like her page on Facebook @catsteinbooks.

Also by Catherine Stein

The Earl on the Train

An earl with a problem.
A woman with a plan.
The journey of a lifetime.

How to Seduce a Spy

A barmaid with a rare talent.
A spy on a mission.
A love neither can resist.

Not a Mourning Person

A determined widow.
An ancient curse.
Crime and passion.

Once a Rake, Always a Rogue

He's mended his ways.
But the woman he can't forget...
Might be his undoing.

Eden's Voice

Football, mechanical dragons,
industrial espionage, sexy romance.
Welcome to fall in Ann Arbor.

Available at your favorite online retailer.
www.catsteinbooks.com

Thank you so much for reading.
If you enjoyed the book and are so inclined, I would love for you to leave a review. Happy readers make an author's day!

I love hearing from readers,
so feel free to contact me on social media, or email:

catherine@catsteinbooks.com